Toward the Light

TALKING STICK #34

Toward the Light

TALKING STICK #34

A publication of the
Jackpine Writers' Bloc, Inc.

The Talking Stick

www.thetalkingstick.com
www.jackpinewriters.com
Send correspondence to sharrick1@wcta.net or
Jackpine Writers' Bloc, Inc., 13320 149th Avenue,
Menahga, Minnesota 56464.

Managing Editors: Sharon Harris, Tarah L. Wolff
Copy Editors: Sharon Harris, Niomi Rohn Phillips, Marilyn Wolff,
        Tarah L. Wolff
Layout, Production, and Cover Design: Tarah L. Wolff
Editorial Board: Marlys Guimaraes, Sharon Harris, Mike Lein,
        Dawn Loeffler, Marilyn Wolff
Cover Photos: Dawn Loeffler

Contents

Contents

Contents

Co-Editor's Note - Sharon Harris
Editor's Choice "April Fools," p.74 by Cordelia Kochmann

I have lived this poem. I am still living it. It was like someone else was writing about my life.

What a sad situation. Having to live away from a person that you still love very much. Something went wrong in the past, something that sent you off on separate paths. The longing does not stop; it does not go away or lessen. Two dozen years now and the feelings are still there. The blame and the hurt dissolved long ago—leaving just a solid fondness.

My ex's birthday is the same as my dad's—so I couldn't forget it if I tried. That date is ingrained in my soul and it does fill me with longing. I do have a number to text and I do, just that one time per year—not wanting to bother, not wanting to be a pest—just to wish a happy day—hoping for a response so I do know he's still kicking. So relieved when he responds and we can text back and forth for a few special moments. Okay then—a deep breath. He's okay; I'm okay.

Am I happy? I'm happy enough, as they say. He is there and I am here with our messy little lives. We walked side by side for many years—now in separate places—but there is a solid ribbon of connection reaching between us—always there.

Co-Editor's Note - Tarah L. Wolff
Editor's Choice "This Paint is for the Living Room," p.68
by Kit Rohrbach

I kept every paint swatch that I used in our home. Some of them I reached for simply because that was it. I never wondered why or tried to put it into words. It just was. And that color that I chose (or did it choose me?) made the room it painted. It was the ONE. No sample necessary, just a gallon of paint going home with me.

Other colors the room demanded whether I liked it or not. And trying to find those were always the hardest because sometimes they weren't even a color I *liked*. I am not a morning person. I am not a sunflower. I am nightshade. I am "sooty lashes" that I painted my master bedroom that some would call gray, others would call midnight, and some others may call a storm at twilight. I am certainly *not* "rise and shine" by Clark+Kensington and my living room found it funny that I thought I got an opinion.

My living room was right. That color was perfect.

Easy or not, whether it even felt like my choice or not, every one of them had one amazing certainty in common. They were all going to better my life with just a trip to the hardware store and a bit of prep. (Even if its repainting the same color; after a few years, it's not anymore.)

We can all agree that "blue" is "blue," generally speaking but what about that blue that I instantly hate? What did that poor color ever do to me? Is it reminding me of something long buried and terrible?

What about that swatch that I knew was the ONE. Is it reminding me of something beautiful from my past? Could colors also be like smells, like that fresh-baked bread that takes you back forty years to your Grandma's kitchen? I wonder what that color would be.

Poetry
First Place "Nocturne," p.1 Erin Lynn Marsh

Erin is a poet living and working in Bemidji, Minnesota. She is the author of *Disability Isn't Sexy* and *I May Never be Able to Stop Writing Love Poems.* You can find her online at erinlynnmarsh.com.

Second Place "Death-feigning," p.8 Jennifer Hernandez

Honorable Mention

"Weightless," p.158 Vicky A. King
"My Elders," p.23 Janice Larson Braun
"If Flowers Forgive," p.120 Charmaine Pappas Donovan
"1x0=0," p.151 Georgia A. Greeley
"April Fools," p.74 Cordelia Kochmann
"Migraine," p.108 Gail Lipe

Poetry Judge—Sarah Ann Winn's first book, *Alma Almanac,* won the Barrow Street Book Prize. She is also the author of five chapbooks, most recently *Ever After the End Matter.* Her writing has appeared in *Five Points, Massachusetts Review, Nashville Review, Quarterly West, Smartish Pace,* and elsewhere. Sarah is the founder and editor in chief of *Painted Pebble Lit Mag.* She's the founder of Poet Camp, a creative community where she leads online classes, jumpstarts, and cozy writing retreats. Find her at http://poetcamp.com.

Creative Nonfiction
First Place "Motherless Child," p.2 Tara Flaherty Guy
Tara is a writer living in St. Paul, Minnesota. Her work has been published in *Talking Stick, Miracle Monocle, Emerge Literary Magazine*, and *Longridge Review*, among others. Tara has a BA in Creative Writing from Metropolitan State University in St. Paul, Minnesota, where she lives with her husband and three geriatric, self-involved cats.

Second Place "Grandpa," p.9 Dan Crouser

Honorable Mention
"Banshee Keening Prairie," p.105 Dawn Tanner
"The Naughty Shoes," p.167 Roxanne Lien
"The Missing Journal," p.39 Carolyn Jacobs
"Family Tradition," p.51 Laura L. Hansen
"Small Town—Job Interview, Summer 1975," p.75 Sue Bruns

Creative Nonfiction Judge—Julie Jo Larson is an author, storycatcher, and public speaker. Her books, *100 Things to Do in Minnesota Before You Die, 100 Things to Do in Minnesota Northwoods Before You Die*, and *Secret Minnesota a Guide to the Weird, Wonderful, and Obscure* (2026), are published through Reedy Press. Larson allows her sense of wanderlust to lead her on adventures across the USA and Canada. She travels with MsStorians, a band of women who enjoy history mysteries. Their adventures appear in publications across the region. Larson lives in the Brainerd Lakes Area with her husband, family pets, and flock of chickens. Visit juliejolarson.com to learn more about her books.

Fiction
First Place "Rubes," p.4 Sandra Hughes Eberhart

Sandra is a retired English teacher and administrator who could never find the time to write for fun. Now that she is retired, it is one of her favorite activities. Having grown up in Nevis, Minnesota, and lived and worked in other communities, she is happy to reside in Park Rapids where she enjoys her children and grandchildren. Being a part of *The Talking Stick* has been a goal of Sandra's since she asked Linda Henry to teach a class on writing and publishing while she was community education director for the Park Rapids schools. Out of that class came the Jackpine Writers' Bloc, the group that started *The Talking Stick*. She is so pleased to see a seed she tossed into the wind still flourishing all these years later.

Second Place "What's Mine is Yours," p.11 Chris Marcotte

Honorable Mention
"The Sullen Sisters," p.65 James Walsh
"Churros," p.81 Dan Crouser
"The Choice," p.115 Tammy Tisdell
"Granny, Death!" p.31 Ryan M. Neely

Fiction Judge—Pequot Lakes author Candace Simar writes historical fiction set in Minnesota and North Dakota. Simar has been blessed with awards from the Western Writers of America, Women Writing the West, Laura Awards in short fiction, Midwest Book Awards, Will Rogers Gold Medallion, Western Fictioneers, as well as regional awards. She is a grateful recipient of Five Wings Grant funds.

Creative Twist
First Place "The Quest," p.6 Steve Linstrom
Steve lives in St. Paul and is an active member of the West Side St. Paul Writers Group. He has published two novels and several short stories including stories in *Talking Stick Vol. 19* and *Talking Stick Vol. 33.*

Second Place "The Promise," p.14 Tara Flaherty Guy

Honorable Mention
"Saturday's Child," p.67 Margaret Hasse
"Disgust," p.86 Ann Marie Newman
"Number Five," p.53 Jayna Locke
"Ever After," p.89 Jennifer Hernandez

For the *Talking Stick*, we've created a separate category called Creative Twist. Writers could use any form of the eight words but had to use all of the words in each submission. The winners and honorable mentions were chosen by the Jackpine Writers' Bloc Editorial Board.

The words this year were: *lantern, iridescent, stark, damp, coincidence, broken, blistering, bound.

Toward the Light

TALKING STICK #34

Erin Lynn Marsh . *Poetry (1ˢᵗ Place)*

Nocturne
after Li-Young Lee

Erin, be aware there will be people
out to hurt you, even in the constellation
of your own family. Mind, the sky is vast
and there are many stars to choose from.
Constellations will overlap. The blade of the warrior's
axe is also a flower petal in a little girl's bouquet.
You are the cartographer of your own night sky.
You will find stars hidden behind planets
and name them after children you have loved.

Erin, do not feel lonely when you realize no one knows
the real you. You cannot possibly keep track of who
you are from one day to the next. Label folders
with your alternative names and fill them with charts
and calculations—send them to NASA. They will know
what to do. People will watch your path across the night
sky and ascribe meaning, say you do it all on purpose.

Erin, you are brilliant. You pulse
and flash with great ferocity. You are the star
the sailor searches for and follows all the way home.

Tara Flaherty Guy . *Creative Nonfiction (1ˢᵗ Place)*

Motherless Child

My memories of that late fall morning are not of any conversation, nor exchange of information, nor even probable cause of death. Instead, there is just a dizzying rush of images, some frozen in my mind as sharp and clear as ice sculptures at a buffet, others as misty as a boneyard in a vampire movie.

I do have a clear memory of picking up the ringing phone that morning and hearing my younger brother's voice telling me that our mother had died in the night, but only a hazy recollection of the words I said back to him, something along the lines of *oh my god no*, or *how did it happen*. I recall a vast tilting of my world —almost physically, as if there were new asymmetrical slopes and valleys at weird angles along the familiar old pathways of my life.

I drove the road to my folks' home that morning, traveling it for the first time as a motherless child. My only distinct memory is of sitting in my car at the interminably long red light near their house, without any recall of the traffic or road conditions or route I had just driven to get there. Just a dim understanding that the dear and familiar landscape of my life had changed forever.

When I reached the house, I made my way to my dad through the friends and neighbors who had already started to gather. The Ryans from next door had come first, after Tom Ryan went out to get the morning paper and saw my dad sitting in his underwear on our front steps, crying. He called the St. Paul Police, who notified my on-duty brother. He sped in his squad car, lights, but no siren, to his own childhood home—a surreal drive, he would later tell me. Racing to emergencies—and often finding a newly-dead person when he got there—was the stuff his job was made of. But this time he was racing to the side of the woman who had pressed a radio to her belly while pregnant with him so he'd always love music, who had nicknamed him "Butchie" as a little boy, who had taught him the ukelele. Mom was gone by the time he arrived.

In the house, I found Dad sitting in Mom's recliner instead of his own, one of the shabby, matching tan corduroy pair they'd had forever. He looked so strangely out of place, so terribly alone and unbalanced in the living room that had given my life symmetry and order since childhood.

I went to him and knelt before him, laying my head on his heaving chest. He was inconsolable, seemingly unaware that I was there. His white T-shirt was damp underneath my cheek, from sweat or tears, or both. His heart was pounding so hard and so arrhythmically that I suddenly panicked, imagining that I might lose him too—he'd had heart trouble for years. Shaking, I rose from his side to go phone his doctor to ask for some kind of medication to calm him.

With my call completed and my cousin en route to the pharmacy, I returned to kneel at my father's side and remained there; it might have been days that passed then, for all I knew. Eventually I noticed Mom's TV Guide folded open to yesterday's schedule—to the last shows she would ever watch—lying on the little footstool next to her chair. Underneath the stool were her sneakers. *Whatever will we do with her tennis shoes?* I wondered stupidly. Stricken by the sight of the little white shoes, a dark flower of grief bloomed and burst in my breast. I put my arms around my dad again and wept.

"No one will ever love us like she did," I said, laying my head on his chest. But my father didn't answer.

Sandra Hughes Eberhart . *Fiction (1ˢᵗ Place)*

Rubes

He was old. His friends were old too and didn't have the energy needed to notice much of anything anymore. They gathered each morning at the local bar for coffee rather than alcohol. A time for gathering together. When lonely old men could flirt with a young bartender who would smile at them. Where they told stories of a bear that came through their yard last night or a car that just wasn't running right. Each looking for something that connected them somehow. A time to feel like they belonged. People who would share their lives.

And then one morning Rubes didn't come into the bar. The others noticed and remarked on it, but no one considered checking to see why his stool at the bar was empty . . . his cup sitting ready because the bartender had put it out in the spot he always took. It wasn't until several days had passed that they really took note. It was the young bartender who decided they should maybe check on their friend. She sent the part-time deputy out to see if he was okay.

Meanwhile the men at the bar avoided talking about him or his absence. It was as if they felt it would make it real to talk about the possibilities. They knew that each of them could be the one who was no longer sitting at the bar each morning. They didn't want to think about why he wasn't there. They didn't want to look at the empty stool. No one sat on it. The bartender had stopped putting out his cup. They talked and slurped their coffee and joked with the bartender as usual.

After an hour or so, news came back from the deputy that their friend had been found. They waited for the words. Each of them knowing that the words would not be good. Their friend hadn't gone to visit family or taken a spontaneous trip somewhere. He hadn't been visited by his kids or gotten into a project. They knew he was like them. If he was able, he would be there with them. They hoped time would freeze and the story would end differently.

The deputy's words were delivered to a silent room. Men who didn't look up at him or at anyone else at the bar. They already knew, but the words cut each of them. And when the deputy had given credence to their fears, he turned and walked out of the bar. No one moved. No one spoke.

And then, just like that, they all went back to their talk of deer counts and auction sales while secretly they were thankful it wasn't them.

Steve Linstrom . *Creative Twist (1ˢᵗ Place)*

The Quest

The Explorer paused outside of the entrance of the cave and breathed in the stale, damp air. Who knows when the last person dared to explore the forbidden passages? Only someone with his extensive experience could be trusted with the task and he was bound to successfully complete it to further enhance his reputation.

The darkness closed in behind him as he moved into the chamber. The glow from the small opening near the roof of the cave provided a ghostly hue to the chamber.

He lit his lantern and held it over his head. It put an eerie glow on the ancient artifacts littering the crevices in the wall of the cave. Who knows how long they had been there, broken and forgotten by civilizations long past?

Still, there was no sign of the object of his quest. Nothing was ever where it was easily reached. He took a deep breath and acknowledged the stark reality that his search could not be completed without delving deep into the dark recesses.

He'd have to be careful, very careful. A cave-in was always a dangerous possibility. Holding his lantern high over his head he peered into each of the dark crevices, cautiously avoiding any unnecessary movements.

There! He spotted his goal. High on the wall, it was barely visible. He thought that it was no coincidence that it was hidden behind a strange golden orb. It could be a trap.

As he held the lantern high over his head, the light turned the bubbles blistering the surface of the object into iridescent pools of light. Standing on his tip-toes, he reached deep into the crevice following the arc of light to move the orb ever so slightly, so delicately, to reach the object of his quest gleaming in the darkness.

The orb came loose and rolled directly toward his face. Stretched out with the lantern over his head, he was unable to move completely out of the way as the orb rolled closer. He dropped his lantern, sending it clattering to the floor and dodged the advancing orb. He lost his balance and fell back to the floor of the cave, hoping that the entire wall before him wouldn't follow the orb and crash down upon him, burying him in this remote cave forever. Deep within the walls of the cave the *boom, boom, boom* of ancient drums reverberated around him.

A female voice from above filled the chamber.

"Darn it, Billy," the voice from outside the entrance said. "What's all that racket? I sent you down to get Grandma's candy dish a half an hour ago. What are you doing down there in the dark?"

Billy pulled himself off the floor and turned the light switch to the basement storage room on. He pulled the candy dish off the shelf and retrieved the still bouncing basketball, putting it back into its place.

"Sorry, Mom," he said, picking up his Junior Explorer flashlight from the floor and flicking it off. "I'll be up in a minute."

"I ask you to do one thing and . . ."

"I got it, Mom," he said. "It's right here. Stuff fell."

"You better not have broken my mother's dish! I told you to use the stepstool."

"Relax, Mom, it's covered in bubble wrap."

"You know, you've spent the entire summer with your nose in a book. Fourth grade will start in no time and you've hardly been outside. Get out the house and go play. Use some imagination, for goodness sakes!"

Billy flicked off the light switch and closed the door to the storage room.

The last whiff of the dank smell of the cave reminded the Explorer of adventures to come.

---

lantern, iridescent, stark, damp, coincidence, broken, blistering, bound.

Jennifer Hernandez . *Poetry (2nd Place)*

Death-feigning

The frenzied bark of my shepherd mix
in the back corner of the yard at 3 a.m.
has me pulling on a coat over my pajamas,
hurrying through the mud,
trying not to slip and fall.

Soon she'll have
the whole neighborhood awake.

At the back fence, she's standing on hind legs,
paws up, peering over, body quivering,
high-pitched yips insistent. I shine the flashlight
from my phone. Not five feet away, balanced
atop the neighbor's chain link, is a possum,
naked tail pointed skyward.

I tell the dog to hush, try without success
to slip my fingers underneath her collar,
quiet her excited cries. The possum,
of course, does not move.

And even as I chase my dog around the shed,
heartbeat racing, half-slumber gone, I feel
such a bond with that fat gray possum. I know
that fear, sharp teeth so close you can hear
them snapping. That silent screaming need
to run, the frozen limbs.

But also,
the strength it takes
to stay perfectly still,
wait it out,
survive.

Dan Crouser . *Creative Nonfiction (2ⁿᵈ Place)*

Grandpa

As Reggie curled into his bed for the night, I leaned down as I've done a thousand times and patted his head. "You're a good boy," I said, as I've also done a thousand times in the years since we brought him home from the Humane Society. But on this night, the action and words sent me spinning through time and space, landing me in Cleveland, Ohio, summer of 1966, on the sunny front porch of my paternal grandparents' apartment.

I believe Dad brought just little brother Mike and me on this trip. Not Jenny, who at eighteen months old would have stayed home with Mom, and certainly not Pete, who wouldn't be a gleam in our daddy's eye for another few years. Just the three of us guys, visiting Ann and Dick, a.k.a. Grandma and Grandpa Crouser. My one and only clear memory from that trip places me with Grandpa on the porch of their unit in the fourplex, known as "The Ruth," where they had lived since before our daddy was a gleam in his own daddy's eye. Mid-1920s.

Dad always described Grandpa as being a pretty good guy despite not having had a lot of breaks in life. By 1966, after years of breathing bad air at the enamel factory, his lungs had about had it, and as far as I could see, playing there at his feet with a truck or something, he must have been nearly as old as God Himself. In my memory, he sits on the davenport, watching me play, watching traffic rumble down Detroit Avenue, thinking about—what? Life? Death? And as I look up at my ancient progenitor, he leans down and pats my head with a beatific smile that hangs above me like a benevolent crescent moon.

"You're a good boy," he says.

And that's it. That's the entire memory. I'm pretty sure that was the moment when I formed the image of God that would live in my mind for many years—a gentle, kindly man, older than Time, smiling down on me as if to say, it will all be fine; in spite of everything, it will all be fine.

Only years later did it occur to me exactly how old

Grandpa was at that moment, just a year or so before he died. Born in 1904, he would have been all of sixty-two years old that day. I wonder how he would seem to me now, if I could somehow visit that porch on that day, sit next to that pretty good guy on the davenport, and see him through my sixty-four-year-old eyes?

Since that's my only clear memory of that trip, it's also my only clear memory of Grandpa. I surely wish I had more of them. But at least in the one I do have, he's smiling at me, and I'm a good boy.

Chris Marcotte . *Fiction (2nd Place)*

What's Mine is Yours

The dead usually leave something intriguing behind and my aunt Rose was no exception. My cousin Micki asked me to help sort her mom's personal papers. I told her I'd bring scones. Micki *always* had coffee and usually chocolate.

My cousin and I were close. We were born just a day apart, while our fathers were overseas. Our mothers, Rose and Violet, had married brothers which made us double cousins. Micki and I both had blue eyes, dishwater blonde hair, and a handful of freckles. Micki was taller than me and wore glasses, but it was clear we shared family characteristics. Occasionally, someone thought we were siblings which made us smile.

Micki was an only child, and my sister had already moved out, so I was kind of an only child too. Our families lived in the same neighborhood. My cousin and I played together, graduated together, and even now, we got together once a month.

"Clara." Micki hugged me close. "Thanks for coming over."

"No problem, you helped me with my mom's—"

"Haul boxes to Goodwill? That, was easy." Micki slid the raspberry white chocolate scones on a plate, handed me a mug, and nodded towards the coffee and Godiva truffles. "Help yourself."

She knew my weakness. "Are the truffles to make sure I stay?"

Micki wiggled her eyebrows Groucho Marx style. "I know this isn't an easy task, and I really appreciate your help."

I laughed when I saw the kitchen table. "Some things never change." At each end there was a document box three-quarters full and in the middle a couple of baskets. Micki was Miss Organized.

She took another bite of her scone. "Yum. You should seriously consider selling these—I'd be your best customer."

I smiled. I did love to bake. "So, how do you have this set

up?"

Micki licked the tip of her finger, dabbed scone crumbs, and brought them to her mouth. "Probate is done, therefore I'll shred bills. The baskets are for items to look at later."

We began to sort. Occasionally one of us would share something—a "Family Circus" cartoon, a recipe torn from a magazine, or an unfinished crossword puzzle.

Over lunch I pulled a letter from the basket. "This is from my mom. Can I read it?"

Micki swept her hand above the table. "What's mine is yours."

"It's from right after we were born," I said. "My mom says she checked at the courthouse and the birth certificates were fine, so Aunt Rose didn't need to worry."

"What's that supposed to mean?"

I shrugged. "Who knows? Your mother was a bit of a worrywart."

"That's for sure." Micki grinned. "Remember the time we went to our first boy-girl birthday party in fourth grade?"

I giggled. "She told us about spin-the-bottle but forbade us from going into a closet with a boy. That game was so old-fashioned—and boys that age had cooties anyway!"

Late in the afternoon Micki waved a piece of pink paper. "Wow, here's something I didn't know—according to this my ma paid the midwife who delivered twins for your mother on August 22, 1944."

"I had a twin?" I grabbed the receipt. "Two girls." Tears gathered without warning, and I quickly wiped them away.

Micki squeezed my hand. "That must have been hard for Aunt Violet."

I nodded, not quite ready to speak.

"I don't think I told you," Micki said, "but years ago, Ma shared that she'd lost two babies before I came along."

"Oh, how sad—for both our moms." I reached for Micki and smiled. "But thank goodness, you *are* here and that we lived so close."

Micki handed me a truffle. "I'm the lucky one."

As we continued sorting, I pondered the new information. I had been told that my dad and uncle had entered the service about the same time, and I know I was conceived just before Dad left.

"Do you know what time you were born?"

Micki chuckled. "Sure, ten minutes before midnight."

"Me, at 12:15 a.m." I started to speak, shook my head, then said, "Do you think possibly—?"

"*I'm* the twin?" Micki pushed her glasses up on her forehead. "No way."

"Mom would've known Aunt Rose lost her babies. Maybe when she knew she was having twins she decided to give her one. I can see it."

"But what about our dads?" Micki asked.

I smiled. "Think about it. By the time the war was over, and they were home, we were walking."

"So, we really are—"

"Sisters," I said.

Micki grabbed my hands. "Not, just sisters—we're twin sisters!"

We danced around the kitchen like happy young children.

Tara Flaherty Guy . *Creative Twist (2nd Place)*

The Promise

She faces east into the night wind, standing high above the place where the restless sea and the dark land crash and tumble together in a tumultuous embrace. At the bottom of the rocky cliff she can see the surf churning against the rocks in the shallows, all frothing white lace and iridescent turquoise in the eldritch moonlight. Her lantern is at her feet, her hooded wool cloak is beaded with moisture. It does little to protect her from the raw night air which is damp, scented with sea and salt and memory. It is not mere coincidence that she has chosen such a bright, clear night to stand on the cliff. Behind her she hears Leannán nicker, stamping his front hooves, impatient to be done with this strange errand, this danger, this risk. She has looped the reins from his bridle over the broken branch of a sea-blasted tree that is as white as bone, well back from the cliff, anticipating his anxious worry for her. From childhood the horse has been her heart, and she his; her whole life long they have galloped in wordless companionship along this very cliff through the blistering days of high summer, through the hoary white frost of winter. She speaks back over her shoulder to reassure him. *"Beidh gach rud go maith, mo cuishle,"* she calls. Bound to the branch, Leannán whinnies and chuffs at her voice, breath steaming, but he ceases stamping. She turns back to stare out at the dark sea, willing her love to come, to see, to find her on the moonlit cliff, waiting. As promised. Above her in the ebony cathedral vault of the sky, a shooting star blazes a fiery path through its lesser fixed and placid sisters, then it is gone. She closes her eyes, a ghostly image of the star and its fragile, glimmering trail fading behind her eyelids. Like the hope in her heart, she thinks in a moment of sad, stark clarity, her breath catching in her throat. A vast bubble of sorrow rises and bursts in her breast like a black flower. Still, she will wait. If he lives, if he comes, he will find her there, waiting. As promised.

lantern, iridescent, stark, damp, coincidence, broken, blistering, bound.

Amelia Colwell . *Poetry*

Joy Box Lions

Miles and I have a clear, glass,
gold-framed shadow box
we call our joy box.
It's full of tiny treasures
we've collected from experiences and trips:
a spiral conch shell with the image of
a North Carolina lighthouse we climbed together,
all 220 steps upward into the salted air.

On our way up, Miles, age four,
repeatedly asked people descending,
"Are there lions up there?"
They laughed and assured him no.
I realized at some point that when my dad
told him there would be long lines
to get into the lighthouse, he heard "lions."
And he was still eager to climb the steps with me
to see the view of the ocean because that's who Miles is.
He picks up the shell from our joy box
and says, "Mama, I can hear the ocean."
He's right, you can.

Janice Larson Braun . *Poetry*

Solitaire

To avoid thinking
I lay out the cards
Over and over again,
Red, black, red, black—
Nothing but pain, grief, pain, grief.
I can't shut down the feelings,
Just the thinking.
But I try.
I need to learn to be happy
By myself.
Maybe just content.
But peace is hard to find
In the midst of grieving.
So I play mechanically—
Red, black, red, black,
Seeking refuge in the numbness of numbers.

Jayna Locke . *Creative Nonfiction*

When Time Stands Still

Though nearly a quarter century has passed, that afternoon is seared into memory like a cattle brand. My friend Claudia and I are driving along the freeway. There are technically five of us in the car, though if we got pulled over for some violation, the cop would only see the two of us. The reason is that, between us, we have three babies on board. Claudia is at the wheel because I'm hugely pregnant with twins and can no longer get close enough to the steering wheel to get my feet safely on the pedals.

This is humorous in the abstract, and incredibly annoying in reality. I can't go to the store for milk. Can't tie my shoes. And of course, Claudia has to drive when we visit our doula.

In one earth-shattering moment, however, all of this will cease to matter. These things are petty. Immaterial. They are what one might call "first world problems."

When the accident happens, we are talking about mundane mom stuff. How we manage discipline issues with our three-year-olds, perhaps. Or how to get them to eat their vegetables. Or the fact that even though they are only three years old, they are best friends who play house and doctor and make gifts for us out of Play-Doh.

And then she screams. And time stands still.

I grab the door handle, look all around us—in slow motion, it seems—and step on a brake that doesn't exist on the passenger side. I'm certain we are about to die.

"Oh, my God," she says. "Did you see that?"

"Holy crap. No. See what?"

She glances between the road ahead and the one in the rear view mirror. "Accident. Horrible, horrible accident."

I turn to look backward the best I can, being pregnantly obese and all. There are dust clouds. Cars are careening off to the side of the freeway to avoid the collision. And then it's too far behind us to see anything more. I turn back.

Claudia has gone stark white. She has witnessed death. She tells me there is no doubt in her mind.

"We just missed it," I say. "If we were just three seconds further back, that would have been us."

We are silent for a bit, absorbing this.

"There are five people in this vehicle," she says. "Five souls."

The gravity of it all hits me full force. I begin to cry. I cry for those people. And for the three babies resting warm in our bellies. waiting silently for their time to enter the world. And for how truly powerless we are to protect them.

Then I take her hand. And we drive the rest of the way like that, holding tight until time once again moves on.

Audrey Kletscher Helbling . *Poetry*

Up North at the Cabin

Orange fires the morning sky,
blazing light onto Horseshoe Lake
in northern Crow Wing County
where I discovered Up North at the Cabin
well into my sixties.

Until then, I knew nothing of cabin life,
of dense woods and pristine water,
of haunting loons and lazy afternoons,
of bare toes in sun-warmed sand,
of jack pines stretching toward the stars.

Now my northwoods experiences
write stories of summer days
with the grandkids gathering shells,
pinecones, and memorable moments.
Together—laughing, learning, loving.

Stories of dining lakeside,
of circling the campfire
to roast marshmallows for s'mores,
of folding ourselves into a hammock,
of caring not about time, only place.

This place. Up North at the Cabin,
where sky, trees, and water meet,
where family centers the world,
where we fish, swim, and imagine
bears roaming the woods while we sleep.

Joni Norby . *Creative Twist*

Spirits

Spirits are not bound by earth,
but found playing hide-and-seek
in the iridescence of hummingbird wings,
or swirling in blistering desert sands,
or dancing in damp morning mists.
Spirits sweep away the stark and broken bits
of our hearts.
It's no coincidence we follow lantern light,
it captures spirits' glow, pathways
to our ancestors' souls,
to the hope of an afterlife,
to be set free.

*lantern, iridescent, stark, damp, coincidence, broken, blistering, bound.

Charmaine Pappas Donovan . *Creative Nonfiction*

Old Red Rug

A preoccupation with the whereabouts of a missing rug has taken hold of my aging mind. This family rug, used as a blanket, was a band-aid for family ailments. Its redness reflected the blood of our heritage. Wooliness made it heavy, bulky, and scratchy. Only when family members were sick did it come out of hiding. Then it was thrown over the ailing person to break his or her fever and heal with its weight, reputation, and sheepish smell of lanolin. I spent a fair amount of time healing under that cover's warmth while I swam through tomato juice dreams.

Perhaps the wool yarn was dyed red as a symbol of Christ's blood—like every Greek Easter egg I ever cracked open. They were always dyed a deep red. Whoever possessed an intact egg after participating in the annual cracking contest, saved the sturdy, unblemished egg on a shelf for good luck during the coming year. My Yaya also wrapped a coin in waxed paper and baked it in bread. This offered another opportunity for year-long luck during Greek Easter.

I asked my younger sister if she knew what happened to the blanket. She never answered me regarding its whereabouts. It's a mystery. Although I helped dismantle our parents' house, I do not recall seeing the rug. I would remember that. It was very distinctive, not only because of its weight and color, but also because of its hairy look. The rough yarn was pulled through the woven square throughout. These yarns stuck out about three inches all over the top of the rug/blanket. We often called it the bear blanket. It was one of a kind. Which made it all the more precious.

And where did it come from? I vaguely remember the priest coming from Duluth when I was eleven to bless our house. He sprinkled holy water in each room. He chanted in Greek and waved a frankincense decanter back and forth as he walked through the house in his shiny official robes. Could this have been when the rug appeared? Or did Dad's sister Urania bring it back from Greece on one of her year-long trips to visit her in-laws? I don't know. I have no recollection.

I miss that strange and special rug we used as a blanket—lost in the shuffle of life, the passage of time. Suddenly I miss that blanket like I miss the way my parents are gone from the everyday. Perhaps they will explain the red rug's origin to me at some future date—when it is my turn to be gone—when I am missed in the passage of time, lost in the shuffle of life.

Janice Larson Braun . *Poetry (Honorable Mention)*

My Elders

It is important
For me to believe
Trees have memory—
That as they stand stoically
At the crest of the hill
In the frigid morning air,
Enduring fierce north winds.
That they remember
They can survive.
That they know just how
To stand and bend and accept what is.
I want to believe that they take heart
When the February sun
Sparks a lone chickadee's song,
And we all know
The warm days are coming.
And I want to believe
They know me
When I lean into them
For support.

Yvonne Pearson . *Poetry*

Remembering Home

In summer, the morning sun
leaped on our lake's waves.
The moon, beaten into gold,
became a ballroom floor.
Sometimes little pinpoint stars,
hot coals, dropped one by one
into the water, and you could not
know what was up
and what was upside down.

In fall the lake caught fire,
the glassy surface shirred with
flames of oak and aspen, maple,
leaves transmuted into molten gold,
copper, brass, and bronze.
Each day a changing piece of art
pierced our hearts with longing
for what would soon be lost.

In winter from the window
the ermine white lay undisturbed
as fairy dust, erased all boundaries
between the earth, the sky, and us.
The lake was just a darkening,
frozen two feet down, the windowsill
a frame that held all life in stasis.

In spring, the ice broke into
crystals, tiny towers, chiseled
flowers. Gave way to lily pads
like freckles on the water, a promise
stamped on greening eyes and mailed
us every summer.

Chris Marcotte . *Fiction*

A Riot of Color at the End of the Road

"Mom, are we almost there?" I kicked a rock with more force than needed. I hated going along to help. Mom insisted we all had to walk to the end of the road. Our new neighborhood was hot, sandy, and full of sticker weeds. I would have rather stayed home. I had just gotten the hang of dot-to-dot and wanted to finish coloring a picture of flowers.

"Just over this hill." Mom gave the wagon with the two babies a two-handed tug. "Be careful," she called to my younger brother and sister.

"I see a—" my brother was cut off by frantic barking.

Behind a picket fence surrounding a small white house, a large black poodle pranced about. I heard, "Down, Ricky, down," before I saw who spoke.

"Hi," we hollered.

Through the fence I saw flowers everywhere. Many more than in my dot-to-dot garden. And like the sixty-four crayons I got for Christmas, there were at least three shades of pink, red, purple, and yellow.

"I'm Buzzy," Ricky's owner said. She opened the gate and reached out her hand. "Please come sit and tell me who you are." We followed Mom like fuzzy ducklings and settled near her and the babies on the grass.

Buzzy plopped into a sagging lawn chair and lit a cigarette. I glanced at Mom who thought cigarettes were disgusting.

"My name is really Iola," she said, shooing the smoke away. "But my grandson came up with Buzzy because the bees are always buzzing around me and my flowers."

I grinned. This adventure was getting interesting. Mom introduced us as her five stair-step children, ages six months to almost six years. She explained that we had moved into a house down the road.

"I bet you're parched." Buzzy's eyes twinkled. "I've Kool-aid and cookies if it's all right."

"Only if we can help," Mom said.

"Sure." Buzzy looked my way. "Tina, come along, then."

In her kitchen, Buzzy blew crumbs off a plate and handed it to me. She nodded towards an old-fashioned cookie tin.

The cookies were as big as the lid on an oatmeal box. While Buzzy made a pitcher of Kool-aid, I asked, "Why is your house so small?"

"Used to be a chicken coop. My son turned the coop into a house for me."

I smiled at the stacks of books and magazines, the jungle of plants, and the knick-knacks in her living room. I liked it, though Mom would call it cluttered. And I liked Buzzy.

After our snack, Buzzy took us into her garden. She rattled off names I'd never heard of like tiger lily, forget-me-nots, and bachelor's button.

I stood by some tall leafy plants with tufts of bright red. "Oh, I like these flowers best of all."

Buzzy grinned. "That's bee balm, and the bees love them!"

An hour later Mom was ready to go. "Thank you, Iola, for such a fun afternoon."

"Come anytime," Buzzy said.

I lingered at the gate. I wondered if I could return on my own. Buzzy was nothing like my parents. And I liked that.

"Can Tina stay a minute? I've something to give her."

I crossed my fingers. "I'll run to catch up."

Mom sighed. "Okay."

"Thanks," I said. "I'll be quick!"

Armed with a paper bag and a shovel, Buzzy led me to another patch of bee balm. "I've got lots of this." She placed the soil ball in the bag and handed it to me.

"Thank you." The red tufts tickled my nose. "Buzzy, you have such beautiful flowers." Saying her name tickled my lips.

Buzzy smiled. "It's because my yard is mostly chicken manure."

"What's that?"

"Chicken poop."

I wrinkled my nose. "You mean poop makes flowers grow?"

Buzzy nodded. "It makes all plants grow, and it's not just chickens, but cows and horses too. The manure sits for a few years, loses its smell, and becomes rich black dirt."

"And the flowers like it."

"Indeed, they do." Buzzy laughed. "As much as you kids like my sugar cookies!"

I giggled.

She poked my arm. "I've a word of advice—don't give your mom such a hard time."

I was astonished she knew how I felt.

"It's not easy being the oldest, but with five of you, she needs your help. It's just the way it is."

"I know."

She patted my back. "Come as often as you can. I think we'll become great friends."

Beaming, I started down the road. "Thanks for everything!"

I already *knew* Buzzy was my friend.

Sharon Chmielarz . *Poetry*

Recipe for a Wilderness Experience on a Long Summer Afternoon

What if you placed a tin camp mug on top of five books. Unevenly stacked, they're rocky cliffs. The mug tips. Its coffee overflows as dusky waterfall, a scenic and culinary marvel steaming down the books' cliffs into your cup. *Au lait!* The cream you've always felt eluded you in life circles big as an islet graced by its own tiny tree shelter. Pine and cottonwoods. What's more, that blue camper—charming. Go ahead, open the door; yes, it's yours! Try it out. Lie down. Take a nice, long afternoon nap in it if you want. Maybe you'll want to go swimming in the lake or floating or tanning on the dock. Take a dip? a sip? Or, just watch birds wheeling overhead in that big, clear, wonderful summer sky. *Or,* read! At least for an hour or two? You reach up to the stack to try another book. And down it falls! Wow! *Summer Magic*: the title knocks you over.

Cathy Wood . *Creative Nonfiction*

One Should Never Eavesdrop

There's some low ground between the hayfield and the lake where crooked box elders have grown into a tangle. Several of the dead trees have fallen partway, but are hung up in the living. Today the wind is blowing heartily and as I walk past the tangle, I am stopped by the many voices of the shifting trees.

I can hear a bow drawn slowly across violin strings; an old trunk lid creaking open; a frightened puppy whining; the single tock of a grandfather clock; tennis shoes squeaking on a gym floor; a porch swing, gently swaying back and forth, back and forth. Suddenly, there's the sound of overall, widespread, chortling. I glance around suspiciously.

It would seem a joke has been told.

And I think it's on me.

Susan McMillan . *Poetry*

Off Road

I want to say my favorite color
is blue.
     My eyes are blue,
so this is how I see things

but instead, I ought to tell you
it's like the earthworm's dirty brown,
     or expectant eyes
of old, devoted dogs

or maybe yellow,
like fried-egg faces of tickseed
that flutter in seduction
     of leggy soldier beetles,
but no.

And not blush, burgundy,
     or claret, either, but a
hold-it-right-there
stop-me-in-my-tracks
downright bull-fighting red

     like the sexy flash
of Flame Red paint
on the first Jeep I had—

feisty 4WD,
     gas-greedy monster
for all that off-road cruising
I never did.

Ryan M. Neely . *Fiction (Honorable Mention)*

Granny, Death!

Ethel woke to a strange woman standing over her bed.

The fog of sleep drained from her mind and with it the temporary confusion about where she was.

"Hospital," she said.

The woman smiled. "You're awake. Do you know what day it is?"

Of course she did. She remembered everything. "October third."

"Good," the nurse said. "Can you remember what happened?"

A car accident, you dolt. Ethel lifted her hand to her head and traced a finger over a bandage. "I . . ."

The nurse smiled sadly. "I'll get the doctor."

Ethel forced her eyes wide, willing them to water. "Vernon—?"

"He's hurt," the nurse said, "but he's alive. Across the hall."

Ethel let her hand drop to her mouth.

Once the nurse was gone, Ethel flipped back the blankets. She scowled at the hospital gown.

No pockets.

She unplugged her monitor, hung her IV bag from a hook there, and rolled the contraption to a cabinet across the room.

Inside were her things.

She picked at the stitching on a hidden pocket in the bottom of her purse. From there, she retracted a syringe carrying a teaspoon of clear liquid and placed it in the basket beneath her monitor. It blended nicely with the blood pressure cuff there.

Ethel slipped from her room and wheeled her monitor across the hall.

She had a job to finish.

Every door down the corridor was closed and featureless. *Goddamn HIPPA.*

Vernon lay inside the room of the second door she tried.

His face was mottled black and yellow. An IV tube swept over the bed rail before disappearing under the blankets. An oxygen tube routed over his lips and disappeared into his nose. His own monitor beeped an erratic rhythm.

Ethel reached for the syringe. She held it between two fingers and a thumb and was surprised by the quiver in her hand.

She was also surprised by the tenderness she felt for the man lying before her. She wanted to stroke his hair. Nurse him back to the vigorous man she had fallen in love with.

The syringe balancing on her fingertips contained her trademark concoction. The reason her colleagues had given her that terrible moniker.

She was eighty-four when she had finished her last job. Age had stolen her strength and speed and had given her cataracts, making it impossible to use her sniper rifle. She hated that she had been forced to turn to poisons.

She had hoped to never do this kind of work again, but that was before her great-granddaughter had come into her bedroom after a "day out with Pop-Pop" and had whispered those devastating words.

Ethel's mind rejected the idea at first.

It wasn't until she saw her daughter's expression that said, "We thought you were getting it worse than us."

The table beside Vernon's bed was already littered with cards from the Elks Lodge.

Ethel couldn't reconcile the man she knew with the monster the women of her family had exposed. She wanted to defend Vernon. Prove that they were wrong.

A black cage enshrouded one of Vernon's arms. Pins drove through his flesh. He wore a neck brace, and a catheter tube slipped from beneath the blankets.

Tears pricked her eyes and old feelings tightened her chest.

Here lay the man she loved, beaten and broken and bowing down at death's door.

Maybe pulling the emergency brake had worked after all.

Maybe there's no need for—

Vernon shifted.

His eyelids fluttered and his gaze locked onto her.

His good hand patted the bed. "C'mere, darlin'." The words were muted and mumbled, but she had heard them a million times and they had always made her heart flutter.

It couldn't have been Vernon. The girls must have been mistaken.

Vernon patted the bed again. "Don't worry, nobody has to know."

Ethel's heart stopped.

Every moment of training—decades of silent wet work—rushed back to her in an instant. She was no longer Ethel Bracegirdle. Once more she was Granny Death.

She sat on the bed, plucked the IV tube from beneath Vernon's monitor, slid the syringe into the injection port, and slowly depressed the plunger.

Tears caressed the contours of her cheeks.

When it was done, she took a breath.

She wiped her face on her hospital gown, stood, and made her way to the sharps bin on the wall.

She dropped the syringe inside.

Then she opened the door and stepped out.

She had just settled into her bed when the alarm sounded.

Meridel Kahl . *Poetry*

Blue Violin

On a November-gray day,
somewhere in a grocery store parking lot
violin music pierces chill air
with memory wrapped in loss—
afternoon tea served in paper-thin china cups
a sunlit room with people, now gone.

Pulled by the sound
I search the lot
until I stand before a father
in a heavy woolen coat
with enormous lapels
and his son whose slender fingers
speak the strings of a blue violin,
the color of forget-me-nots.

I stand speechless
as the day weeps.

Steve Linstrom . *Creative Nonfiction*

Ditch Creek

You didn't fish for brook trout in Ditch Creek; you hunted them. The creek was only a few feet across and, despite its unappealing name, it wound beautifully through a pine forest, forming little pools of water so clear and shallow you could see the brookies along the sandy bottom. The pools seemed like they were only a foot deep but one time I was messing around with my little brother and fell into the ice cold water. It was really over three feet deep and soaked my shoes and jeans. Dad gave me hell for it; I guess he was probably right to. It was just him and me and my four-year-old brother staying in a little trailer at the edge of the camp ground in the most remote part of the Black Hills near the Wyoming border. A bunch of wet clothes was just one more thing to deal with.

It was the spring after my mom died of breast cancer and Dad was managing alone with a nine-year-old and a four-year-old.

We always camped in the most remote corner of the Forest Service campground. Other campers tended to cluster near the pit outhouse. Dad was a high school Physics teacher and dealt with people all school-year long. When we camped, it was just us.

Dad showed me how to fish for trout in Ditch Creek. You had to sneak up on them. If you stood on the bank, they could see you through the clear water and would hide. Even if they stayed in the shadows of the pool they wouldn't bite if they saw you or even your shadow. Most of the best pools were protected by pine boughs arching across the entire creek. Crouching on the bank or behind a tree, you had to hold your pole high with the bait in your hand facing upstream. Then you let the line, weighted with light split shot, swing out giving it a final little flick while pressing the spool release to get under the pine trees into the current. If you flicked too hard the line would snag on the pine canopy and never hit the water. Too softly and the line would plunk behind the fish and the pool would be ruined for an hour or so. If you did it just right, you could watch the corn-baited hook tumble along the sandy bottom of the stream, coming to rest just below where the trout were holding themselves against the current. Then you'd wait until one of them would slowly dive and kind of sniff at the corn. Eventually, the yellow of the corn would disappear and you'd give the line a little jerk to hook the brookie.

They were beautiful, iridescent rainbow-colored with dark spots and bright white bellies. Out of the water, they looked nothing like the dark brown logs of fish swimming against the current. They were usually six to eight inches long and slick with mucus. I was always careful to never touch them unless my hand was wet to protect the mucus. Dad gave me a pocket knife and taught me how to gut and clean my own catch.

We had trout for dinner almost every night. I don't think Dad knew how to cook anything else but hot dogs and SpaghettiOs. After dinner, we'd play Crazy Eights. Dad built a card holder out of two by fours so my little brother could play too. That's the way we spent most of that spring and summer.

Dad got remarried the next winter so it wasn't just us anymore. We went back and camped at Ditch Creek a few times, but the Forest Service thinned out the pine trees near the creek. It ran faster, cloudier, and was easier to fish. Anybody could do it.

Everything had changed.

Sharon Chmielarz . *Creative Twist*

One Creative Twist
". . . Who Hung the Twinkling Lanterns in the Sky . . ."
Edward Taylor, 1642-1729

It's no coincidence that we're still enchanted by night's lights in the otherwise stark, coal-dark universe. Broken though we may be by daylight intrigues, earthlings are still fascinated by a limitless sky that provides its own tiny lanterns. Yea! The heavens haven't abandoned us yet. Earth-side we can't feel the stars' blistering heat; stars are a boon to us down here. As night watchers, we're bound to their fascinations. It's no coincidence that iridescent stones, like diamonds in earrings, are especially desirable facsimiles. As for that stranger's tearfully damp eyes? By night they become "twinkling lanterns," too.

*lantern, iridescent, stark, damp, coincidence, broken, blistering, bound.

Meridel Kahl . *Poetry*

Chipping Away
for my mother

A weak winter sun casts
milky light into the living room
of your tiny apartment,
reaches you in your chair
me on the sofa next to you,
my hand on your arm.

Loss, your constant companion,
joins us—your husband, my father, died first
followed by two of your life-long friends.
You can no longer travel, write letters, drive,
walk around the neighborhood.

You say, *Thank goodness,*
I can still read.

We sip our tea,
not knowing
a throng
of invisible marauders
has already launched
its first assault on your eyes.

Carolyn Jacobs . *Creative Nonfiction (Honorable Mention)*

The Missing Journal

Oh, my gosh. Where's my journal? I'd just gotten through TSA at O'Hare and noticed a different, something's-missing feeling, when I donned my backpack for the trek to my gate. A quick unzip and search through its small interior left me dumbfounded. A cursory look and sweep of my roller bag came up empty too. Now, observing through some odd sixth sense, I saw myself frozen in backtracking thought, with searching eye movements and lower jaw dropped and paralyzed. Where was my journal? How did I miss packing it this morning?

I traced it back to the hotel suite's coffee table, where earlier that morning I expounded on the topic of philanthropy. I'd recently been contemplating the vastness of unmet community needs, and my wish that more people would speak openly about the value of giving. In my leisure that morning I probably set the lovely, leafy-green bound book down as I tended to other things like packing and morning mindfulness. Mindfulness, right.

Now my mind was recalling exactly what *was* on the pages that a stranger could now be reading. I'd written about my mother, who at age eighty-five had had her fourth facelift, and when I'd seen her recently I was in shock . . . the same word that perfectly described her eyebrows' frozen expression. In my discomfort at looking at her, my journal was the non-judgmental confidant that received my inner hope to drop my judgment and resume an easy, loving relationship.

I remembered writing while sitting alone along a quiet creek at Zion National Park, as two deer meandered nearby. I reflected on what I called *my* Zion, my very favorite place on earth, and the four times I'd had the good fortune to be there. Somehow being alone at the creek transported me down memory lane, and, with journal at hand, I sat on my ergonomically comfortable rock and wrote.

I have a box of old journals at home that currently sit in torch-limbo, not knowing what I want to do with them. Should they be kept for finders to read? For my sons to hear what might be a one-sided account of my life in those distraught times I was drawn to write? Or might I choose one last read-through, followed by a ceremonial fire, sending my past up in flames and ashes blowing in the wind? All this purposeful pondering for these protected pages that I've now negligently left in Chicago, which feels like an intimate piece of my heart is in a stranger's hands. Or, perhaps, in many strangers' hands, such as the Housekeeping Department of the Warwick Hotel on Michigan Avenue.

As I let my mind roam through thoughts of anguish and dismay and concern for the not-yet-remembered, terribly personal entries possibly hidden in those pages, somehow a cleverly positive counter-notion appeared: Maybe my journal was making the rounds in housekeeping, and it's a good read. Perhaps someone feels a little bit better by knowing *this* stranger struggles similarly. Or maybe someone else decided to really smell the roses, in their neighborhood or in a far-away place like Zion. And possibly a person or two may dig deep into their pockets to help uplift a segment of their community.

I will wait and see if I'm reunited with that lovely book of mine. The front desk lady I spoke with as I walked in shock to my gate at O'Hare said she'd try to locate it and have it sent. I know I will breathe a little sigh of relief when it comes, but if it doesn't, I will keep close the notion that others' lives may be awakened in a good way, and my anonymity will be a sweet mystery.

Deborah Rasmussen . *Creative Nonfiction*

Why Folks Hang on to Old Stuff

One summer, between college years, I processed address changes for a mid-sized magazine. Not the worst job I ever had—glad I didn't have to sell anything—but it was boring to clip old address labels, attach them to files of readers who had moved and agonizing to write out all those new street numbers, new cities, occasional name changes. When my hand began to ache, I began to wonder why folks hang on to old stuff, like this particular periodical, for example. Why not drop it, try something new, I grumbled, massaging my fingers and forgetting about Whitey and Brownie, two threadbare stuffies who for twenty years had lived everywhere I had lived. Many jobs later, many moves behind me now, those cuddly pups still share a shelf with faded photographs, musty books, and dust-covered collectibles, every day, without fail, renewing their subscriptions to the story of my life.

Charles Kausalik-Boe . *Poetry*

Under the Bough

The neighbor's central air conditioner hums.
Come, sit with me on my porch
and enjoy the summer heat
in spite of the droning sound.
We will share cool water and lemon bars
to quench our thirst and needs.
Let us read *The Rubaiyat of Omar Khayyam*
indulging ourselves with verse
from foreign lands and times past
feeling the gentle breeze
shaded under the red maple bough.

Janet Kurtz . *Fiction*

"It Starts with a 'C'"

"I believe her name starts with a 'C'," she mused, stuck in the middle of her sentence. "You know her," she continued. "She worked at the school when you were still there. Her husband sells real estate. They have two daughters. The oldest is at the University now. She's doing a semester in Spain. In Granada. I think you had her in your Spanish class." She looked into my eyes hoping for a glimmer of recognition.

The conversation comes to a complete stand-still, going down a detour intended to recapture the name of the key character without which the point of the story would be lost. This only increased our determination to identify the subject of her vignette.

"Were her girls on the basketball team?" I interjected, trying to help solve the mystery. "Both really smart kids?"

"Yes, that's the one. The daughters' names are Sue and Luann. Sue was in the same grade as my son, but why can't I remember their mom's name? We used to be in water aerobics together on Wednesdays and . . ."

"Are you sure it starts with a 'C'?" I interrupted. "That might be throwing us off."

"Well, I guess it really doesn't matter. We both know who we are talking about. I suppose it will come to me in the middle of the night and I'll have to give you a call." She finished with a sigh.

"Anyway," she seemed headed back to her story, but paused, then moaned, "I forgot what I was going to tell you! It must not have been very important. This is so exasperating! It's happening to me more and more these days."

"Just a minute, before you give up. You were talking about the upcoming fundraiser at your church. You were listing the volunteers already signed up and what they were going to do," I added, hoping it would revive her tale.

"Of course," she continued, rolling her eyeballs toward

the ceiling, perhaps expecting to find the answer there, before returning her conversation to the woman whose name began with a "C."

"We need more help in the kitchen. She is the best. A good cook, organizer, and just always knows what to do. I'm hoping she'll be interested, but I can't call her if I don't remember her name!"

"Wait, wait." I stopped her. "The last name is Isaakson. Her husband is Charles. Charles Isaakson!" My brain now worked backwards using his name. "Charles and . . . Charles and . . ."

"I have it!" I exclaimed. "You're talking about Sharon! His name starts with a 'C' and hers starts with an 'S'!" I clapped my hands together, feeling like I had won the lottery.

"Of course, Sharon!" She grinned. "At least that 'C' came from somewhere. This brain fog stuff is so exasperating. Lately, I often catch myself with only the first letter of a word as a clue. I'm amazed at how much we all know about someone as we dance around in circles before arriving at that one name we need." She smiled.

"Well, now you can give her a call and see if she is available to help you," I offered. "Who else do you have working?"

"The Crafty Ladies are handling the Christmas sale section. They are so talented. They do rosemaling, crocheting, quilting, and others will do a bake sale. One of them is an expert lefse baker. She has three kids and lives out on the lake. Her husband teaches Driver's Ed. I believe you know her." She grinned. "I think her name starts with a 'C' . . ."

Joanne Esser . *Poetry*

Nothing is Stationary

Even when the wind goes still,
water keeps folding itself
over itself
meditatively
in layers
toward the shore
again
again
again

Charles Kausalik-Boe . *Poetry*

One Summer Afternoon

Weeds have all but overtaken
my backyard gardens.
Spring rain brought
green beauty to the world
and weeds of all sorts.
Trying to pull them out,
I feel overwhelmed, frustrated.
Thinking of Buddha,
I've decided to let go,
let the weeds be.
I relax, the earth smiles
and somewhere a goddess
laughs.

Marlys Guimaraes . *Creative Twist (Poetry-haibun)*

One

Mornings were the best. You, a master of breakfast cuisine. The smell of coffee. Toasted bread. Butter blistering in a pan waiting for fresh cracked eggs brought in from the chicken coop. Scraping sounds of butter being spread across toast. Sometimes the burr of the coffee grinder. I'd round the corner, smile, wait for your return smile. I'd long ago learned that a "good morning" greeting would not be returned.

It was no coincidence that we were together. Me, a broken vessel bound by traditional rules. You, a quiet man who understood the value of silence when turmoil threatened. You were a lantern, a light with an iridescent shine in the stark, damp world.

Two cups sat on the table, small cafezinhos. Always two. Always waiting for my sleepy, pajama-laden body to arrive. We didn't need words on those early mornings. A smile, a gentle touch, or a lingering hug was enough.

the silence of your
empty cup
a lone wolf howls

---

*lantern, iridescent, stark, damp, coincidence, broken, blistering, bound.

Donna Isaac . *Poetry*

Lonely

Think of all the songs about loneliness. "I'm so Lonesome I Could Cry," good old Hank and that whippoorwill. "Eleanor Rigby" with her face in a jar by the door. Three Dog Night with "One is the Loneliest Number." Green Day's Armstrong's shadow is the only thing that walks beside him. Loneliness sits in the same place as grief, a lump in the heart. People are not meant to be alone-alone. Solitude is something else. Emerson says to seek it in the stars. In New York, little table lamp robots are now keeping lonely elders company. I guess that is better than nothing. *Lonely* is sad—all those soft *l's*, that long *o*, like a deepdown moan, gray rainfall, a Shakespearean invention. Lonely is like endless drops of water eroding the seconds away.

Bernadette Hondl Thomasy . *Creative Nonfiction*

Sunday and The Paper

My affection for the Sunday paper began in the 1960s on a Minnesota farm. When the *Minneapolis Sunday Tribune* arrived, it felt like a basket of exotic fruit had been delivered to our rural home. News of books, travel, state, national, and world events waiting to be consumed. The fresh newsprint and tempting headlines were irresistible.

When times were good, we had the Sunday paper delivered. But often we drove nine miles to Owatonna to buy the beautiful bundle of news because Dad needed to look for something in the Classified Ads section. Machinery, livestock, straw, fence posts, etc., for sale throughout the tri-state area. Mom and we three daughters delved into all the sections—fashions, features about Minnesota and far off places, recipes, comics, weather, gardening, and even some obituaries proved interesting.

This newspaper fascination eventually led me to write for my high school paper, earn an MA in journalism and work as a staff writer for the *Toledo Blade*. During the next decades, the Sunday and daily *Toledo Blade* were essential reading for me and my husband. He absorbed every inch of the sports section. I relished Sundays—my time to feast all day on the features and photos assembled on life in Toledo and beyond.

Then came retirement and a move to California. Within our first few weeks, we were engrossed in the daily and Sunday *Sacramento Bee*. How else were we going to find out what was happening in a city and region that was brand new to us? We learned about persimmons and pomegranates, parks, politics, people, restaurants, beaches, redwood trees, and local sports. *The Sacramento Bee* was a good instructor.

That is until a few years ago when costs became exorbitant. We compromised by only subscribing to the beloved Sunday paper. But still the $700 per year package for the Sunday paper delivered and required digital package felt over-priced. Plus, delivery was spotty.

The final aggravation—relentless quarterly cost increases. Each time we complained and negotiated. *The Bee* would offer us another "deal" supposed to last for a year, but as soon as the quarterly electronic payment came due, it jumped beyond the price we had been quoted.

The breakup was messy. We canceled twice, each time receiving an additional bill for $16.15, even though we had paid in full for all the issues that had been delivered.

Then, the annoying sales calls started coming to my husband's cell phone. I groaned one day when he announced, "Oh, I got a deal for the Sunday paper. We can start getting it again." Just when I thought we had made a clean break.

After three months of somewhat erratic delivery, again the price increased. I called to cancel, again.

Our final plan was to purchase the Sunday paper occasionally, like my family did when I was growing up. A drugstore on the way home from church was handy. But on the first Sunday we discovered that the store had not carried *The Bee* for several years. "Everything's online now," the cashier said.

But worse news lay ahead. Glaucoma and macular degeneration had decreased the vision in my left eye; I could no longer read the small newsprint without my eyes aching and tearing up. I could barely look at the Sunday paper for ten minutes before giving up. The joy of discovery was gone. No more obits, book reviews, comics, interviews, letters to the editor, local news.

I am sad that my love affair with the Sunday paper is ending. Yes, I can read some content online; I can report headlines to my husband. I can try to use a magnifying tool to read the physical paper occasionally. But Sunday will never feel quite the same.

Laura L. Hansen . *Creative Nonfiction (Honorable Mention)*

Family Tradition

Mother darned holes in socks. She saved bacon grease and wrapped up leftovers, no matter how small, in enough layers of aluminum foil that I imagined them having the half-life of plutonium. I suspect that deep under our county landfill there are little silver packets of edible food. Even now, I can see her sizing up a sliver of ham, a stringy slice of beef, and some teaspoon-sized bites of potato for our next meal. Sometimes, late at night, I would sneak to the fridge and toss them in the bin just so she wouldn't make some strange soup for lunch the next day—*turkey and pork in chicken broth with leftover rice and potato warmed up with a quarter cup of mixed canned vegetables.*

The memory of it still makes me shudder.

And those socks she darned with hefty cotton thread! Goodness. She would worry over and over the hole, cross hatching and weaving, until the patch was solid as a steel grid fence. You would put on those socks, and it was like having the end of a ball peen hammer stuck in the toe of your shoe. She wasn't a hoarder, mind you. We didn't have a massive ball of string in the drawer or piles of old magazines. Darning socks and saving leftovers were her specialties.

My problem is worse. I have the inability to throw out poems.

My phone's memory is taken up with poems the way other people's phones are overloaded with photos they never look at and never print. Except I print those poems, too. I have stacks of them, piles, boxes, binders full. I can't explain why; it's not like I'm going to make them into a stew or wrap them in foil or weave them into sturdy toe-pinching socks. But I can't let them go. Can't bear the thought of them at the bottom of the landfill. Better to burn them, I think, and set them free on the wind or scatter their ashes across the water.

Someday I'll let them go, but for now I'll wear my poems like old socks. I'll feast on the last of my words.

Dawn Loeffler . *Poetry*

Tomorrow's Yesterday is Today

I had a haunting dream last night
of Freedom and Death

It came that way:
first Freedom,
then Death quickly after

Almost as if it had no choice
A reaction to an action
One pushing the other into existence

As if, such joy could only be contained
in the earth and air
And we should only be allowed a glimpse
of its magnitude, at the end

As if, after having delicately nibbled
its morsels through the journey
a cool drink of water was needed
to wash those morsels down
clearing the way for Death to breathe
through the long hollowed-out space

What a waste not to have gobbled
large chunks along the way

Jayna Locke . *Creative Twist (Honorable Mention)*

Number Five

You step out into the night, the lantern's glow showing the way. A train makes its sorrowful call in the distance, and you wish for a moment that you were on that train, riding somewhere. Away.

You walk toward the pond and the woods, the sack under one arm, the other consigned to holding the lantern aloft to illuminate the path. It is a soft and soundless night, but for a smattering of unharmonious crickets that seem tentative, unsure of your intent. You find your footing on the broken ground, carefully stepping over dark roots and rocks along the little-used trail.

Oh, how you imagined a small herd of children running here on summer afternoons, their laughter echoing up into the trees and dispersing like butterflies. Fishing in the brook that feeds the pond. Leaping from a swinging rope into the pond's deep center. Shouting and splashing.

On school days, they would have packed themselves onto the bus that trundles along the country road at the end of the drive. They would fight sometimes, and you'd have to break it up. Or yell at them to clean their rooms. There would be drama, like someone using the last of the peanut butter. Drinking straight from the milk carton. Even this you crave. All of it.

Stupid, unruly dreams.

The pond is iridescent in the moonlight. No coincidence, perhaps. The moon's pull seems powerful enough to be the cause of this loss and its blistering ache, taking what does not belong to it. Again.

At the pond, you skirt around to the north, careful in the boggy damp not to sink into mud and slime—for, when this is done, you want to return to the cabin clean and unburdened. Light as dandelion down. Washed like a brook stone.

A mossy stump marks the spot where you turn into a tiny glade. And there, at the base of the twin pines that share a common root, you lay down your bundle. The sack is bound with twine. Inside, a soft towel swaddles the little form. The one who tried so hard to stay.

You lift the towel bundle into your arms. Imagine warmth. A soft coo. But no. It is cold.

There is movement on the path, and then *he* is there. A warm hand on your shoulder. Then a shuddering embrace.

"This one too," he says. And his eyes glisten like the pond in the lantern light.

"Yes." You close your eyes. Hold the bundle close just a little longer. "Number five." You cannot give her a name, for a name would tear you asunder.

He has brought a shovel, an implement you forgot in your haste to leave for the woods unnoticed. Though perhaps a strong stick would suffice in the soft loam. You nod to him. Words are insufficient here. There is no sentiment that will do. No prayer. Nothing to fill the space that is infinitely deep and wide.

Silently he digs an earthen cradle near the others, each sweetly laid to rest in the twin pines' shade. And you lay the bundle in.

Then he carefully fills the hole and pats the mound.

"Oh God," you whisper. "My heart."

"Mine too, my love."

You douse the lantern. The moon now hangs dull and yellow in the sky like a failing flame. The night is stark and deep all around, like a black hole in the universe. And you could be falling away into the void of the darkness and the endless sea of stars. Nothing to catch you. Nothing to hold onto in the vast space and the blackness.

An owl calls. *Who-who-who.* Another answers. And you find your feet again on the ground.

He reaches for you. Holds you. You sway in each other's arms. You come back to yourself. Back to him.

"We have our *one*," he says.

"Yes," you agree. And you smile. "Perhaps he is enough. Our wonderful boy. Thank the stars he doesn't know."

It is time to return home to him. You think of your son,

your prize, in his little bunk, sleeping sweet sleep. Perhaps dreaming of the brothers he hopes one day will come. How he will teach them to catch fish in the stream, to find frogs in the pond and capture fireflies in a jar. And also, to be careful in the woods and in the water. To keep safe from harm.

If only he could keep them safe.

*lantern, iridescent, stark, damp, coincidence, broken, blistering, bound.

~   ~   ~

Peggy Trojan . *Poetry*

A Connection

What I said
was not as important
as the fact that
you were listening.

Laura Krueger-Kochmann . *Poetry*

truth or fear

my little dog crouches under an end table
every piece of fur on her body visibly shaking
as thunder rumbles above us
delicate ears alert and twitching
        this is what fear looks like

the big and unknown
surrounding you with noise
it's hard to find rational thought
amidst the crash and boom

my thunder
a scrolling list of potential disaster
unfurled in my brain
at 3 a.m.
        fire, pain, loss, death, failure
        even embarrassment
the rumbling wakes me
and follows me through this day

I need the rain
        cleansing the darkness
it works like a magic spell
drips down my cheeks, my nose, my chin
it shifts and reshapes the fear
into truth

Ann Marie Newman . *Poetry*

The Confession

We sat beneath old lady oak trees.
Their knobby limbs whispering
groans beneath the burdensome weight
of their tangled Spanish moss locks.

I listened.
"I'm alone and dying. Cancer."
Still and sultry air, infused with a mist of
salty sea tears bathed us both in sorrow.
"My wife and my children left me.
Years ago, it was.
I run them off with my temper
. . . my drinking . . ."
The old man confessed his transgressions
to me, a stranger he'd only just met.
We were the only people in the park.
On separate benches we sat brutally exposed
to the cruel, penetrating gaze of the sun
on a sweltering, "Florida-hot-as-hell" day.

I listened.
"I'm dying and I gotta do it alone.
I regret how I lived my life and
miss my family, but I understand
why they done what they did."
When at last he fell silent, I understood.
This was the confession of a dying man.
What solace did I offer in return?

I listened.

Marlys Guimaraes . *Poetry*

A Hymn, of Sorts

The earth trembles. Wildfires,
hurricanes, crumbling seashores,
parched earth, polar bears
floating on melting ice caps.

Shhhh. Listen.
There's a hum in the air
harmonious—wistful—
without restraint.

A wisdom song is rising up
like an evaporating mist
seeping across the land.

Our wandering souls hear.
The collective understands.
Though trampled by deniers,
financiers, and orgies of hate,
in the end, truth will march on.

Anthony Anselmo . *Creative Nonfiction*

The Impossible Tree

There is a tree I used to visit every year. It grew along the shore of the inland sea that is Lake Superior. By most people's standards it wasn't much to look at. In fact, if one walked by too swiftly, they'd likely miss it. I don't know if it's even still there, although I hope it is. You see, this tree is rooted deep into a thin crack of bedrock.

Years ago, a seed was planted in this crevice. By a bird, or a chipmunk, or by providence of a favorable wind. But it needed more than just to be dropped here. Thousands of seeds might have found that very crack in the Canadian Shield rock before and never amounted to anything. So how did this particular seed grow into a seven-foot-tall black spruce? There is no topsoil for the roots to run. No soil of any sort. Just bare bedrock common on much of Superior's north shore. To the naked eye it seems an unlikely place for a tree to survive. Other than a frequent dose of fresh water, how do the roots gather the necessary nutrients for growth? How do they extract carbon and nitrogen and phosphorus? Elements needed for the process of photosynthesis. This, to me, was long a mystery until I happened upon the answer in a college textbook. And if I'd acquired no other knowledge there, at least I discovered some secret to life. How to grow and live in the harshest conditions. That, I think, is one of the most profound lessons I might have learned. And it wasn't even on the test. That tree is living proof that one can plant their roots in any environment and survive.

So it is that the seed must have found respite upon some clump of moss or lichen where there was moisture and nutrients enough to blossom. Lichen is a composite organism made up of two separate organisms, algae and fungus. This unlikely partnership can sometimes provide the necessary environment for a seed to take root. Under stressful conditions, roots grow outward toward any source of nutrients. They may follow the crack in the rock, growing and seeking and fanning out along more cracks, soaking up any available nutrients provided by lichen and algae. These root masses are often larger than the tree on the surface, who might stay small. A smaller, stouter tree has better odds to face the elements. Less likely to blow over or be affected by droughts and storms. Even so, one would not expect a tree growing on rock to live long, but there are examples that state quite the contrary. In fact, some of the oldest living trees in the world planted their roots in rocky environments.

It stands to reason, perhaps there is something to living like the black spruce and the Yogis, who need the smallest of portions to become nearly immortal, stretching their roots so deep they but survive off the dust of ancient clay, molding not their exteriors but their souls so that universal wisdom is enough to curb their appetite.

Knowing this, one can begin to see how I favored that gnarly black spruce. Its height and breadth above the surface will not reach as far and wide as others. And to the common man, what is another but their external appearance? Perhaps just one in a thousand today care how beautiful the soul is or ponder the mysterious workings of nature. But, to me, there is something to be said about the roots which grow deeper and spread further. These special ones are often seen alone on rock-strewn promontories or cliffs where few others are as hardy as it. It has space to witness all things and, with its roots growing deep into age old bedrock, must reach and hold some primal knowledge of the beginnings of time.

Susan McMillan . *Creative Twist*

A Single Yellow Bulb

in a cobwebbed lantern
breaks serenity of the kitchen,
      blisters clutter on countertops
with iridescent light, spatters
the pattern of windowless walls
too close and closing.

Hands bound by age, idle in a lap
on a corroded chrome-legged chair
whose riven vinyl cushions
      reek of neglect—

hands knotted and white,
palms stark in this aura of gold,
empty of tissue or tool to clutch,
      empty of any use
except to map the dry riverbed
of a long life line.

Passion abandoned. Hope
diminished by day, as hours linger
and fade.
      Each minute
demanding the same dull wait.

If only, by coincidence,
a door might yet open
      to some small purpose or change,
an iota of self-worth could be regained
and a flame lit in two damp eyes
now languishing in lemon haze.

*lantern, iridescent, stark, damp, coincidence, broken, blistering, bound.

Dorothy Schlesselman . *Poetry*

This Late November

Metallic tang of snow in the air.
I cut down woody stalks
of a three-foot basil shrub,
remembering summer's
tender leaves in pasta and pizza.

I'm bogged down in my body,
always aware of the incision
in my left breast—healing,
though a dull ache reminds me
it's only been one week.

Pathology results mixed,
I face more surgery:
a lymph node biopsy will show
whether cancer cells have spread.
Hard to think of anything else
in this bardo state of waiting.

Dusk falls.
Snow begins to collect
on marigold blossoms, still
improbably huge and golden
in this dim twilight.

Rebecca Rae . *Creative Nonfiction*

Breakfast in the Snow

One morning when I was eight or nine, I was sitting at the breakfast table. Outside, the frozen white landscape taunted me. Old Man Winter tapped his icy fingertip against the glass, curled it slowly, the way the principal did when he called Ritchie Nordstrom into his office. The aroma from the toaster that had heated my Pop-Tart begged me not to go.

They used to make Pop-Tarts without frosting and, wouldn't you know, those are the kind my mom bought. I hated them, but back then kids didn't complain about food.

Nibbling the edges bought me some time, but my mother calling, "Hurry up, you'll be late for school and if you haven't finished your breakfast, take it with you!" cut short my delaying. How did she know? Her head was buried in the closet, her hands appearing briefly tossing mittens, scarves, and hats over her shoulder.

I scrutinized the pale rectangle, dry as the pages in the books waiting for me at school. There wasn't enough milk left in my cup to wash it down. I would have to take it with me. On the way to school, I could just toss it.

Mom zipped my coat and tied my poofy fake-fur hat that resembled an oversized pom-pom. Wearing crocheted mittens, I fumbled to grasp the handle of my pink checkered lunchbox with one hand and my crumbling Pop-Tart with the other.

Winter stung my eyes and slapped my cheeks as I crunched my way across the front yard to the road that led to school.

I considered dropping the unappetizing pastry on the road but pictured someone driving around town with a square chunk of dough stuck to their tire and they'd figure out it was mine. I scanned the scene for a hungry stray.

I'd almost reached the river and my hands had started to sweat inside my mittens. Once over the bridge I'd be halfway there. Then, I'd only need to cross the RR tracks and highway; a few more blocks and I'd be at school. I trudged along, jittery when cars passed, sure someone would notice me dropping crumbs on the edge of the road.

On the bridge, I decided to pitch it over the rail into the river. Wait, that wouldn't work! My mom, or the police, would spot the soggy, frostingless raft, fish it out, and find my fingerprints on it! I would have to eat it.

"I didn't hike a mile clutching this stupid pastry just to stop and eat it now!" I muttered to myself. Besides, there was too much fuzz from my mittens stuck to it. I'd be picking lint out of my teeth forever.

Closer to the intersection, the Pop-Tart crumbling in my anxious grip, I spied a big bush almost covered by a pile of dirty snow. If snow disguised a bush, surely I could hide what was left of my breakfast there.

I felt guilty the rest of that day. When my teacher called on me, I was sure she'd ask, "Did you finish your breakfast?" On the walk home, I ran past that pile of snow. In bed that night, I laid awake wondering if my breakfast would still be there in the spring.

I never saw that Pop-Tart again and no one ever said a word.

Twenty-five years later I brought my little girl to visit my hometown. As we headed toward my old neighborhood, I pulled over next to a liquor store that stood where that bush used to be and told her the story. She giggled, picturing me in a furry hat, carrying my checkered lunchbox, desperate to find a place to hide what remained of my breakfast.

She looked to where the bush and pile of snow used to be and asked, "Did they really make Pop-Tarts without frosting?"

James Walsh . *Fiction (Honorable Mention)*

The Sullen Sisters

The night had an aura to it, a vibe of melancholy plucked on the low E-string. It felt dark—as if the street lights were out, but they weren't. The chill air was still, quivering slightly but not enough to trigger any further leaf fall. Even the sky was resigned to the changing seasons, and fought back leaden tears. Inside, thermals laced with cumin and chili powder pulsed from the kitchen, beans still bubbling on the stove, and mingled with the cornbread vapors being exhaled by the oven. That was the night they moved in next door: the sullen sisters.

The oldest couldn't have been beyond her early thirties, and the younger probably trailed by only a year or two. But asking an old man to judge any woman's age, let alone those probably a few decades younger, is nothing if not fraught and monstrously unreliable. Suffice to say, they were young enough that the shine should still have been at least partly on the apple of life. That's why their demeanor was so peculiar. So at odds with the vibrancy and optimism of youth. So different than one might expect from young women in the early years of making their way in the world. Granted, some people are born old. But being born old is one thing, and being dyed in ennui is another. And this felt more like the latter than the former.

We came to learn that Crystal was the older sister and Madeline the younger. But beyond names and obligatory pleasantries, no personal information was shared. They came and went, with seemingly little fervor for each other's company or that of anyone else. From all accounts, they were little old women trapped in young women's bodies, moving through their daily routines with the same level of zeal I reserve for colonoscopies. Shuffling to the garage in the morning, returning at the end of the day with a slight, somber slam of the door. The sequence never varied—Crystal's home, now Madeline, now silence until lights out around ten. Even my wife and I showed them up by hanging in until eleven. One thing's for certain, if these gals are representative of their generation, it is very well rested. Weekends, holidays, the pattern seemed as unchanging as the low energy level barely emanating from their abode. We had to wonder: what cataclysm could have rendered these young women so devoid of joy? Did their laconic tendencies stem from some shared, sad event, or was it just a genetic tendency towards deep melancholia?

Nearly a year had passed since their arrival, these two siblings of the apocalypse. My wife and I were out for a walk; the days were beginning to shorten but enough warmth was still being packed by the sun to warrant shorts and sandals. Strolling up the sidewalk, we bumped into Madeline moving from her car to their front door with a bag of groceries. She acknowledged us, barely, and we took the bait by trying to engage in some more extended conversation. But it was for naught. After a hopeful, if awkward, start, we clearly saw her discomfort as she shifted towards the house. Clinging to a shred of hope for the slightest bit of rapport, we lobbed our Hail Mary pass and went on to comment about the idyllic weather—thinking that could provide a pleasant, if somewhat shallow, close to our clipped interaction. She acceded to our meteorological observation with the slightest nod of the head. Then, from nowhere, and for the first time in our experience, a wan smile slowly crossed her imperturbable countenance.

"Summer is ending!" she said, in a tone of well-tempered exuberance, and then ambled with the slightest spring in her step towards her darkening doorway.

Margaret Hasse . *Creative Twist (Honorable Mention)*

Saturday's Child

Her inventory of today's to-dos
lengthens: fix broken fan,

wash bathroom floor, clean
and close chimney damper.

The list, neat as an itemized
receipt, prepares her to act

as a blistering task-mistress,
bound to clutter an entire day

with the mundane, to shutter
the lantern of pleasure with work.

Simply cataloging chores fills her
with stark pride as if she's already

finished the jobs.
Just before she dons old clothes

and gloves, by coincidence
a neighbor calls to invite her

for a walk on this autumn day.
Outside a streaky window

she sees how the trees still shine
iridescent red and gold.

She decides to be like a leaf
and let go.

*lantern, iridescent, stark, damp, coincidence, broken, blistering, bound.

Kit Rohrbach . *Poetry (Tarah L. Wolff's Editor's Choice)*

This Paint is for the Living Room

It's the color of headlights
reflected on storm-wet asphalt.
It's the color of lightning
against an obscure sky.

It's the center of the flame
on a birthday candle

Extinguished with a wish,
flashed past on a highway
driving home in the rain.

Bernadette Hondl Thomasy . *Poetry*

Cross-Stitch Stars

Across a sky of creamy cotton
she stitched thousands of Xs
tiny stars in pale brown thread
constellations that swirled
like Van Gogh's *Starry Night*

What was she thinking
as she worked the needle
hour after hour
on her tablecloth legacy?
Would her children, grandchildren
find their memories and hers
in the cross-stitch stars?

Years later she has joined
the stars shining down
watching her family laughing,
enjoying a meal at a table
draped with her handwork

One by one, they reminisce
recalling her kolaches,
her peach pie, her pickles,
her roast lamb, her loving smile
Yes, her stitches are holding strong

Judy Daniel . *Poetry*

The Pope and I

save rubber bands:
the ones off newspapers, hair,
flowers, asparagus.

It's hard
to throw away anything
so simple, that
holds things together, that
reminds us of connections, of
bonds,
of how hard it once was
to gather things up that naturally
fall apart;
     how stretching bends
into motion,
how the center can fly off,
how grateful we are when it holds.

Marlys Guimaraes . *Fiction*

The Ghost of Machado De Assis

I sat with my back against the wall. The dim light above reflected off the board on the table. I wondered what the next move would be. Would he move his knight in front of my pawn in the corner, blocking my queen? I prayed he didn't see it.

I was playing for money. The winner would take home $5,000. I tried to concentrate on the game and not on the fact that this morning there was an eviction notice attached to my door. Winning would resolve that problem. I had to funnel all my energy and thought processes into the game, remind myself to stay focused, and not allow worry to cloud my attention.

I watched the wrinkled hand of my competitor hover over his knight. His head leaned closer to the board. Putrid breath wafted toward me, and I heard gurgling sounds in his stomach. As he moved his knight in front of my pawn, he looked up at me through smeary black glasses, and grinned. I saw the remains of what looked like French toast tangling from an incisor.

I knew he was trying to distract me and break my concentration. "The board," I said to myself. "Focus on the board and not on him."

I could block his knight with my castle, but would that be enough? I saw that would put me in line of pouncing on his king, but it certainly wasn't a checkmate. He had options. He used them on the next move.

I studied the board for ten minutes, chasing away discouraging images of me loading black plastic bags of belongings into my rusted 1956 Chevrolet. I saw movement out of the corner of my left eye. Suddenly a man with chestnut skin, black curly hair, and deep brown eyes sat down in the empty chair beside me. Shocked, I looked around. No one seemed to notice. The man was identical to the famous Brazilian writer, Machado De Assis, who was the subject of my thesis in college.

His beautiful long fingers reached across the board and moved my pawn, one space. I almost gasped, then remembered a gasp or any sound before the end of the game could result in forfeiture. Then he was gone. When I looked at the board again, the pawn hadn't moved. Was it all in my head? Did I just imagine him?

I looked at my competitor. He was still grinning, French toast still hanging. I flashed my pearly whites back, moved my pawn, and said, "Checkmate."

Sharon Harris . *Creative Twist*

Unplanned Journey

I am walking alone in the damp darkness
wishing I had my lantern,
but I left home with the confidence
that I was bound to come back soon.

my shoes are now broken.
my feet have blisters on top of blisters.
how long will I have to wander
across this stark landscape?

the night is dark and lavish
and curls thickly around me.
it shivers the back of my neck
like a cold finger.

is it a coincidence
that I feel like I had been here before?
in my dreams at night I have wandered
alone at night and full of fear like this.

but far ahead of me now
I see a brilliant glimmer,
some strange iridescent glow
is beckoning me forward.

I think it is possible that I have died
and this is my trip, my journey.
I have left my body
and I am going toward the light.

*lantern, iridescent, stark, damp, coincidence, broken, blistering, bound.

Cordelia Kochmann . *Poetry (Honorable Mention*
and Sharon Harris's Editor's Choice)

April Fools

am I going to have to make a conscious choice
        every year
        for the rest of my life

to look at the calendar and see the date
and think of you
of your birthday parties, of all the jokes
I won't even have a number to text
but I'll have to make the decision all the same
to ignore the pull, the undeniable urge
to not wish you a happy birthday
even though the date is engrained in my soul

will I still feel it at eighty
when life has beaten me down and built me up
will this date still fill me with longing
will I still wonder what you are doing
will I still want nothing more than to reach out
        though you are far across the chasm
        to let you know I still wish you joy
        that I acknowledge you are still kicking
        that I relish it

will the fact that I shouldn't
        still hurt at ninety-five
will I still wonder if you remember mine
        if you think of calling for even just a second

Sue Bruns . *Creative Nonfiction (Honorable Mention)*

Small Town—Job Interview, Summer 1975

I pull into the Standard station after an eighty-mile drive on a ninety-degree day and peel myself off the Naugahyde seats of my '73 Chevelle with no A/C. I change into interview clothes in the restroom.

Outside I first hear the standard response that will define this small town for me.

"Can you tell me where the high school is?" I ask.

The man steps outside, points down the road. "Just past those trees. It's right there."

"Thanks." I drive just past the trees. It's right there.

Inside I meet the small-town wrinkle-suited superintendent, large moles growing on his hairless head. He doesn't greet me with "Hello" or "How are you?" He doesn't stand to shake my hand but jumps right into questions—increasingly inappropriate ones. Like my opinion on the war in Vietnam and what I think about premarital sex. I know the questions aren't legit, but what do you do? Fresh out of college, teacher surplus, first job. His phone rings as I pause before answering that last question. He takes the call, keeps it short while I hope he forgets what he just asked me.

No such luck. He hangs up the phone and repeats the question, but at least the call bought me some time.

"I believe it exists," I say, and leave it at that. He follows with a few more questions.

Without a clue as to his impression of me, I'm sent to the principal's office, where a leather strap hangs on a peg behind the door. It's 1975. Maybe it's just a remnant of bygone days, bygone policies.

The principal says hello, smiles, asks a few questions—related to education, offers me the job. I sign the contract for a long-term sub job—three months, while the teacher is on maternity leave.

I ask him where I might find a place to rent. He tells me

about the motel downtown that has a few long-term stay rooms, just past the Standard station. I drive back past the stand of trees and the gas station and see the motel.

It's right there.

I stop at the motel. No openings for a long-term stay. I ask the man if he knows of any other place.

"Well, Mrs. Gruber has a boarding house. She might have an opening."

"Can you tell me where that is?"

He steps outside, points half a block up the street.

"It's right there."

I cross the street, knock on the door, meet Mrs. Gruber, but she has no rooms available.

"Any idea where I might find a room?"

"Well," she says, "sometimes Mrs. Johnson lets out her spare bedroom. You could check with her."

"Where does she live?"

"She's just behind the Red Owl. Do you know where that is?"

"No."

She takes a step or two from the front stoop and points across the road with her finger bent to indicate "just around the corner."

"It's right there," she says.

I thank her, walk to the end of the block, look down the street in the direction her bent finger had indicated. There's the Red Owl. It faces Main Street. "Behind the store" must refer to the next block up. I walk in that direction. There's a mailbox with "Johnson" on it. I knock at the door. Mrs. Johnson answers.

I explain my situation and mention Mrs. Gruber's name. Mrs. Johnson does have a room she will rent to me and a space in her refrigerator for whatever I need to store in it. She tours me through her small house, points out the room.

"It's right there," she says.

Cindy Fox . *Poetry*

Wallflower

Nowadays girls ask boys to dance.
Twirling bare skin, inviting improper
Advances, unwanted babies, marriage
Proposals doomed from the start.

In the old days, young women and men
Met at dance halls. Gals sat on a bench
Next to the wall. Skirts pulled over their knees.
Sweaters buttoned up to their throats,
Hands clasped in their laps.

Across the dance floor her secret
Admirer walked towards her,
Her heart danced to the tempo,
Her toes wiggled in her shoes,
Her thumbs caressed each other.

He smiled and her hands opened,
Smoothing away invisible wrinkles,
Her thighs tightened ready to stand,
But it was her girlfriend who stood
Up and accepted his hand.

Crushed, her heart dropped a beat,
Dancing a slow dance in her mind.
She unbuttoned her sweater,
Baring a wee bit of skin,
Just enough to be proper.

Steven R. Vogel . *Poetry*

Chevron

I've not heard the geese this year,
dropping their blue notes from overhead
like warning leaflets for the wary.

Perhaps they still will come,
following the arrow south like any wise
creature, bellowing their avant-jazz

as tuneless encouragement, or as calls
for a pond stop. But stopping is no delight,
and there must be a pointed reason—

same for hefting the skies from stumbling
runways. Once aloft, no one steals
their grace, and their commands

are their own as they patch the flyway
with sounds of grit; feathers like prayers:
Catch one falling and you've gaggled

into a mystery that knows
the fields, the mountains, the rivers.
Stroke it on your cheek and hum

the song of wind shear and hail.
Feel the long adventure of running
the free wind with home at either end.

Elizabeth Weir . *Poetry*

Between Hydrangeas and Trust

She stands eight feet from me, a sleek doe,
hide, polished mahogany in evening sun.

She longs to nibble the tender buds
of our hydrangeas; I long to touch

her silken coat, to know the slender
geometry of her perfection.

We stare, immobile. Each assesses
the intentions of the other.

I weigh the pleasure of her wild trust
against seven weeks of lacy blooms

and, quicker than thought, my voice
shouts—"Go forage in the woods!"

A snort, loud as a bark, and she's gone—
moment of possibility—spent.

Kristin Laurel . *Poetry*

Pike

In the dark depths, you waited.
I drift and troll with my goddess queen mermaid spinner:
White-headed, red-eyed, her copper key spins,
twists and beckons you to hunger, calling you to
part and devour the long blonde, blue, purple, and pink-skirted
hairs, wherein lies the hook: *Here kitty, kitty,*
you alligator face, you cannibal, you killer.

You take the bait, which is connected
to the hook, which is connected to
the line, which is connected to my hands;
my rod bending, drops of water
spinning from the reel, as you drag
the boat ever so slightly and I pull you towards me.

You lay half-way in the boat
staring off into space. Biggest fish
I've caught in my life. No net, no pliers,
no gloves. I am stunned by your needle-pointed
teeth, your long dark green body scattered
with circular scales of gold
as you gyrate your tail, splashing up water.
I'm scared you will die.
I hear children laughing at the beach.

You terrify me, you excite me,
no one will ever believe me, I'll
never have another like you
and then you shake yourself free
and slide back down to the water's mystery,
leaving me wordless,
holding the slack.

Dan Crouser . *Fiction (Honorable Mention)*

Churros

As I pulled in, I noticed the old man standing at the end of the parking lot, leaning with both hands on the cane before him. Scruffy locks of white hair curled from under an ancient fedora that almost matched his olive skin and looked as worn as the oversized jacket hanging off his slight frame. We made brief eye contact before I looked away.

My mission was pastries, but the bakery was still dark, like most of the storefronts on either side of it, so I pulled up to a pump at the convenience store at the end. A ludicrous, thoughtless comment had blown up the morning and had me out here seeking churros, my wife's favorite, as a peace offering. Flowers were good for situations like this. Churros were better, and this bakery, Panaderia San Sebastian, had built its reputation on them.

When I finished pumping gas and replaced the handle, I noticed the man advancing toward me. My first thought was flight, but I dismissed the possibility. I needed those churros. I did a mental inventory of my wallet, thinking maybe, if it came down to it, I could slide the old guy a couple of ones, and then he'd leave me alone. First though, a different tactic. Pretending not to see him, I locked the car and strode into the convenience store. Just a busy guy going about his busy day. I'd paid at the pump for the gas, but there must be something I needed from the store, too. Gum! That was it. I was completely out of gum. Good thing I'd stopped here today.

When I walked back out, palming a pack of 5 Peppermint, he stood there on the sidewalk, so it was the same thing in reverse. Busy guy, no time to notice an old, possibly homeless dude with a cane. Life was hard, sure, and I wished the guy well, but I had a 9:00 Zoom call to get home for and crucial breakfast treats to acquire first. Besides, once you made contact, well . . . you just never knew, did you? Better not to get involved.

I moved the car to a spot in front of the bakery. Why wasn't it open yet? Google maps said 8:00, and it was already after 8:30. Just to be sure, I got out and peered in through the window. Sure enough, several racks of doughnuts and bear claws and fritters and churros shone out from the darkness as if imbued with their own divine light. Salvation mere feet away, yet out of reach. And still no movement inside.

The movement that did catch my eye was the reflection in the glass of the old man hobbling across the lot. He positioned himself directly behind me at the phoneless phone booth near the street and took up his former tripod pose, hands crossed atop the cane, like a patient predator waiting to pounce.

Eyes down, I slid back into my car, furtively locked the doors, and considered my options. Keep waiting? Find another bakery? Give up the quest? It was now pushing 8:40, and my vision of arriving home a conquering hero with pastries was fading fast. I pulled up the map again on my phone. *Bakery near me.* The next closest hit was four miles away in the wrong direction, so I sighed and started the engine, resigned to returning home doughnut-less. *But honey, we have a full tank—and look at this nice pack of gum!*

At that moment, a flicker of red caught my eye. Thank goodness! The bakery's "Open" sign was now on, and a woman was unlocking the door. I shut off the engine and climbed out, startled to find myself face-to-face with my craggy-faced pursuer.

I was trapped. Well played, old man.

I reached for my wallet and pulled out a five-dollar bill. For a moment, he looked confused. Then with an amused little smile, he shook his head and continued past. With some effort, he mounted the curb, pushed open the glass door, and shuffled inside. I followed him into the lovely, warm, heavenly scented bakery.

"Buenos días," said the woman.

My fellow customer tipped his hat. "Buenos días," he said, picking up a tray and a pair of tongs and proceeding to pile up the goodies.

Susan Niemela Vollmer . *Poetry*

Shadows

Our shadows leading us down the sidewalk
Differ from those of years ago
Thinner in places and thicker in others
Moving less briskly and stopping more often

They cross cracks in the pavement
Meld momentarily with roadside weeds
Disappear when a cloud sails by
To reappear still moving forward hand in hand

Shelley Getten . *Poetry*

Quack Grass

I alternate between pulling slowly to remove
the long white string of root and yanking it loose
in large clumps sacrificing bits of flower as I go.

I've become sick from my proximity to harmful people.

I pull hands full of sharp green blades,
toss them onto a pile of waste for compost.

I had forgotten how therapeutic
ripping things from the soil could be
as if I were tearing pain and confusion,
frustration from my psyche,
the malicious actions of others
from my screaming memory.

I'm not perfect but I don't understand
the need for hatred, the undermining
of basic human goodness.

The pile grows larger as I make my way around
the far side of the bed, yet I'm only reaching
the edges, have yet to dive deeper into the center
of the oblong rock-garden formation.

But even clearing a small space to allow sunshine
onto inner blossoms, onto lower leaves to benefit
the blooming plant, even this little bit of weeding
has brightened the garden, has provided
a small sense of order amidst the chaos.

Jennifer Hernandez . *Poetry*

Alluvium

Grief stops by
less often now,
or maybe, like
the sound of water
in a streamside home,
flows on unnoticed.

I mean, most of us
don't pay attention
to our heartbeat,
our pulse,
unless it stops.

I still feel that heaviness
certain days, like the river's
run her course, dropped
deposits of muddy silt
in the delta of my body.

But when I get up,
till the land of my belly,
of my limbs,
the rich soil settles,
nourishes new growth.

I cut a perfect slice of melon
the shade of sunrise,
and sweetness slakes a thirst
I didn't know I had.

Ann Marie Newman . *Creative Twist (Honorable Mention)*

Disgust

She'd bound her breasts.
Made them disappear.
The boys had
broken her acceptance
with the budding of her womanhood.
Their lantern-hot stares,
leering taunts,
damp, grasping hands,
had blistered her with shame.
They'd made their move on her
in the crowded hallway
between classes.
Under stark, school lighting
they'd fondled her breasts
awash with primal, prepubescent lust.
It was no coincidence
the iridescent light in her eyes
disappeared that day.
It too was bound tightly.
Hidden away.
Beneath layers of restraint.
Beneath layers of disgust
for being born female.

*lantern, iridescent, stark, damp, coincidence, broken, blistering, bound.

Jodi Schwen . *Creative Nonfiction*

Grandma's House Down the Hill

I can still hear Grandma's voice in my head, from when I was given permission to go down the hill on a too-infrequent visit. "Well, whaddya know, kid?"

Grandma was homebound. She wasn't chubby, or pleasingly plump, but morbidly obese. Her world was limited to gingerly walking on the silvery-gray boards of her weathered dock to check her cane pole, baited with flesh-colored, squiggly worms she'd turned up in the rich black dirt of her backyard. It was illegal to have an unattended fishing pole, but she didn't care. The game warden left her alone. She'd spent her entire life running her former mom-and-pop resort, except that there was no Pop and hadn't been for quite some time.

Grandma's tiny house used to be a lakeshore cabin. Her family moved into it after the lodge on the hill burned down in a tragic accident, involving a kerosene can and my young mother trying to refill a stove. Nothing was saved from their living quarters in the back of the lodge.

The screen door on Grandma's back porch creaked its familiar sing-song as I entered—often carrying a northern pike wrapped in a piece of old newspaper, which Dad had caught that summer afternoon. We always kept the walleyes for our family. Grandma said she didn't like them, but now that I've tasted tender and flaky walleye—melting warm and lake-alive fresh on my taste buds—I think she was fibbing.

As I entered the cabin, the green, thickly humid lake smell faded behind me. Despite the summer heat, Grandma's house was surprisingly cool. The cracked, multi-colored kitchen linoleum joined with worn carpet stretched and nailed over creaking wooden floorboards. Bald down to its backing in patches, the floral design was barely discernible. Breakfast aromas of bacon and eggs and rich, black coffee still lingered in the late-afternoon air in the closed-up house.

Once she asked me to apply pungent ointment to soothe

her bedsores on her lower legs where she couldn't reach. As I gingerly applied the strong-smelling salve, I wondered, briefly, who would do the same ministrations for me some day, when I became old and infirm.

I had no time to think lonely thoughts of aging, as I remembered Grandma's thick, flabby arms that wrapped me in a hug so tight my face squashed against her bosom, giving me a close-up of the flower pattern scattered across the apron she always wore to cover her faded, cotton housedress.

"Well, whaddya know, kid?" she said, matter-of-factly reaching for the electric alarm clock on the knotty-pine shelf, setting it to go off in five minutes so I would make it home on time. She tightened her lips together while she waited—making the tiny, lip-pursing sound that was her trademark.

I stood silently, shifting my weight, not knowing how to answer. I never did. My three siblings and I were well-schooled to not tell Grandma anything that happened up the hill. Since the mysterious rift between her and our mother, we kids, especially, were forbidden to divulge our family's comings and goings. And for a child during a five-minute visit, it was nearly impossible to filter the thought-speech process—screening what I was not permitted to utter. I lived in mortal fear that I would divulge the wrong, tiny detail and my visits with my beloved Grandma would be curtailed, if not ended altogether.

Grandma and her lip-pursing sound could see me flipping through the giant picture book in my mind, choosing which stories were safe and which ones were too revealing. We didn't have dark secrets. There was no abuse, no tippling, not even petty larceny, unless you counted my one-day, light-fingered shopping spree at the ripe old age of four.

I took a quavering breath and stepped onto the tightrope of telling Grandma about the outside world, without compromising our family stories.

Jennifer Hernandez . *Creative Twist (Honorable Mention)*

Ever After

It was bound to happen. I mean, our town isn't that big, and even though I had moved away, eventually I was going to have to come back.

My high school bestie asked me to be a bridesmaid. So I donned the iridescent gown, drank too many shots at the reception, and followed the wedding crowd to a lantern-lit patio bar where the raucous dancing continued under the moonlight.

Was it a coincidence that you showed up that night? Or was it fate, laughing at me? My hair was a mess, damp tendrils escaping from my chignon. I didn't even see you at first. But when I did, your look was blistering.

I knew that I had broken your heart when I left. Many lonely nights I wondered whether or not I had made the right decision. And don't think I didn't feel a twinge that enveloped my entire body when I found myself in your presence, even after so many years.

Now if this were a Hallmark special, or even a halfway decent rom-com, we would have reconnected, stars glittering in the dark sky above. Maybe after a night of rekindled passion, I would have thrown my city-girl dreams to the wind and moved back into my childhood bedroom for a time. Anything to pursue a second chance at first love, right?

But seeing as how this is real life, rather than fantasy, I chose to face the stark reality. You broke my heart, too. Into little pieces that had taken a very long time to heal. And now that I was here, in my shiny dress full of the confidence that comes from taking chances, there was no way I was going back down that path again.

I gave your sour countenance my biggest, brightest smile, and when the DJ played our song, I danced to it with wild abandon. All on my own.

*lantern, iridescent, stark, damp, coincidence, broken, blistering, bound.

James Walsh . *Poetry*

Rhubarb in Late Fall

Elephantine leaves, like forlorn ears
wilted and dispirited

Caress the wind-chilled soil and listen
for the first snowfall

Mottled in sunset hues, clots of maroon
tangerine, fuchsia, and gooseberry

More beautiful in death than in life.

Vivid stalks dive beneath,
transport chlorophyll

Withdrawing as if from a crime scene
to commune with roots, commiserate and plot

Revenge for wounds wrought by winter
and hope held out for spring.

James Robert Kane . *Fiction*

The Little Engine That Could

Murdering husband Robert is not an item on Melanie Radcliffe's daily planner as she awakes on this, his fiftieth birthday.

In fact, her morning begins in the hope that one focused effort might somehow shake him loose from whatever has gripped him ever since he returned fifteen months ago from his third National Guard deployment in the Middle East. Once gregarious, fun-loving and romantic, he has become sullen, abusive, and opposed to counseling.

Her weapons of choice are his favorite foods because she read somewhere on the internet that taste and smell might trigger positive reactions and open a window of opportunity. She begins with a breakfast combo from their early years—French toast, Jimmy Dean sausage, orange juice and coffee—but he shovels it down in silence and retreats to his basement HO-gauge model train room. She initially hoped building it would be therapeutic for him but it became a universe where she is not welcome.

"God damn it," she mutters and a voice inside her head responds. *What did you expect from that slug? A miracle?* But she stuffs that anger and focuses on step two. His evening meal. Shepherd's pie. Prepared from his beloved mother's recipe.

Late afternoon arrives as she tends her stew pot. Potatoes, carrots, onions, and stew meat swim in bubbling juices. Soon it is time to mix the crust and pop the entire thing into the oven to finish, but before doing that she knocks at the fortress door to tell him dinner will be ready in about forty minutes.

He does not answer, which is not unusual, so she cracks open the door and sees him slumped against a wall, his cell phone on the floor just beyond his reach. He cannot speak but his eyes plead, *Help me.* Her first instinct is to grab the phone and call for help, but as she retrieves it, she pauses. Checks to see if he has dialed 9-1-1. He has not.

And in that instant she decides. She has had enough. Is

sick of being trapped inside his hopelessness. Is sick of him.

She tells him this and more as she watches him struggle, as she waits and waits and waits. And when he stops breathing she crouches next to him. Makes sure he has no pulse. Returns his phone to the floor. Leaves the room and closes the door.

She has just returned to her cauldron and is rehearsing her 9-1-1 call while preparing the crust when best friend and neighbor Sharon knocks at her kitchen door and lets herself in.

"Perfect timing," Melanie says before Sharon utters a word. "Do me a favor and go down and tell Robert dinner will be ready soon. My hands are kinda full here."

Sharon does and shrieks and Melanie rushes down. Seizes Robert's phone. Calls for help. Cues up the Bee Gees' "Stayin' Alive." Then she and Sharon take turns keeping the beat, getting red-faced and sweaty compressing Robert's chest. Paramedics arrive and praise the pair's valiant but futile efforts.

Later that night Melanie lays in bed too excited to sleep. "I'm going to get away with it," she whispers from beneath the covers. A bright, exciting, and unencumbered future beckons. Her joy swells.

And then she hears Robert's trains running.

What the hell! she thinks. *That's impossible.*

She retrieves Robert's loaded handgun just in case there is an intruder and, pajama-clad and barefoot, slinks down the basement stairs and opens the train room door. The entire setup is alive. Trains *chug chug* past flashing crossing signals and the rotund station master waves his lantern, as if Robert is right there at the controls.

The room and the entire basement is empty, save for her, yet she has a disturbing sense that she is not alone.

It happens again the next night. And the next. And the next. She has never believed in ghosts but on the next occurrence Melanie screams from bed, "Go away. Leave me alone."

As if in mocking response, Robert's little steam engine goes, "*Toot toot.*"

Quivering with rage, Melanie decides the only way to get rid of Robert for good is to destroy his treasured creation. All she has to do is wait until morning, find his sledge hammer, and swing away.

First light initiates the search, and when she hauls it from its dusty garage corner, it is heavier than the petite woman expects. She drags it across the garage and kitchen floors, struggles to control the handle as the thing thuds down the stairs behind her and stands beside the eerily inert train table winded but full of joyful anticipation.

Lifting the sledge straight up proves impossible so she begins swinging it like a pendulum, gradually increasing its arc, building momentum. One mighty *oomph* gets it above her head but the effort throws her off balance and she stumbles backward. Two more stumbles send her crashing against a wall-mounted clothing rack custom-made with five protruding seven-inch railroad spikes, perfect for holding Robert's railroading outfits. Perfect for perforating her lungs and heart.

She remains stuck to the wall for a few seconds, like some grotesque insect in a child's bug collection, then tips forward and splats face first onto the painted concrete floor. In that death moment the entire train panorama comes to life and Robert's little steam engine goes, *"Woo whoooo!"*

Mary Kay Rummel . *Poetry*

Arrival

A robin is flying after a finch—
the smaller bird
chirping, the other blazing
silent in light-winged chase,
when suddenly, a sparrow hawk
flashes, light brown burn
scorching the air
from which it plucks
like a ripe fruit the robin,
whose cheeps of terminal surprise
twinkle in the silence
closing over the empty field.

I begin to understand
how a poem can happen—
you have your eye
on an elusive detail,
pursuing its music,
when a terrible truth strikes
and your heart cries out,
carried off.
Now birds sing
on little quiver branches
in my skull
and the manic cardinal
whirls out of my ear
in somersaults of song.

Cindy Fox . *Creative Nonfiction*

Feline Devotion

When we pull up to our house, there's a head in the window. I gather a few things from the car before my husband Jim parks it in the garage. I make my way up the front walk. The attentive figure in the window watches my every move. As I near the door, I rattle the keys.

When I turn the key there is an explosion of feline excitement. Roy, our overweight gray and white tuxedo cat, bursts through the door and charges past me as if there is open seating at a Chris Stapleton concert.

"Hello, Roy . . ." I say to the empty air.

By the time the words leave my lips, he is airborne off the front steps, and dashing down the sidewalk toward Jim. He joyfully circles his pant legs, leaning close, breathlessly grateful for his long-awaited return (we've been gone three hours at the most). Like a smitten schoolboy, he gazes up at him adoringly, pining with love in his eyes.

Meanwhile, I stand at the front door feeling like a backup singer for Taylor Swift, utterly ignored.

Then, as if he's just realized it's warmer inside, he rushes back to the house. It is only when I grab a catnip treat that he notices my existence. This is our chance to bond. He stands by my side intently. He whines and dances back and forth in anticipation. Before it even touches the floor, he has his head in the bowl. His snack lasts all of thirty seconds as he crunches down his tasty treat. I pet him while he washes his face with his paws, then becomes distracted. *Where is Jim?* he wonders. In a panic he searches the house and stops by the closed bedroom door. He hears Jim's purr-like snores and settles down for an afternoon nap himself, all while guarding the bedroom door.

I am left standing alone. The Rodney Dangerfield of cat owners, I get no respect.

Dinner is 5:30. All our cats including "Big Boy Roy" eat in the barn. Like clockwork, Roy senses it is time to eat. I open the back door and a wall of frigid air greets me. He saunters lazily into the snowy night following Jim's footprints in the snow to the barn. He stops to sniff the night air a couple of times, looks back at me with his wise old eyes. It's as if he wanted to tell me, before he entered the barn, that he loves me, too.

~ ~ ~

Laura Syrdal . *Poetry*

Symphony of Trees

Silent harmonies
exist in the canopy
awaiting new wind.

Sharon Harris . *Poetry*

Golfing

I do not understand
what people see in golfing
yes, the grass is a gorgeous green,
yes, the pine needles and leaves
echo that emerald color
the crimson flags at each hole
are a brilliant contrast
I can certainly see all that

yes, the course can be lovely
far from highway sounds
so serene, so comforting
yes, it's fun to watch the golfers
as long as they let me
just stay in the cart

I do like to drive the cart
maybe even keep score
enjoying the breeze
I like to just gently roll
up and down the hills

I do like to hear the crisp snap
of the ball as it leaves the tee
a carefully driven ball
gets spooned up into the air
lifted easily to fly far and free

and the best part
is the nineteenth hole
back at the clubhouse
squeezing between your teammates
bellying up to the bar

Joanne Esser . *Poetry*

Improbable

What are the chances

that any of us
would have arrived

whole, breathing
at this precise moment

in time and this exact
place on a small, spinning

planet? And yet,
we find ourselves

here as surely
as the flower

finds itself
lifting from the seed,

perhaps startled
to see what it is becoming.

Rebecca Rae . *Fiction*

My First Novel

I wrote it. I sold it. The publisher flew me to New York for the signing party where I was received into the coveted world of successful authors and assured the best seller list had a spot with my name on it. I ate fancy hors d'oeuvres I didn't recognize and rubbed shoulders with the mucky-mucks in the industry.

After endless congratulations, a limo drove me to the Waldorf Astoria where I was greeted like royalty and escorted up a Titanic-like staircase to my magnificent suite. After a long, deep, lovely bubble bath, I wrapped myself in a plush, dazzling white robe and nibbled chocolate-dipped strawberries while I gazed out the lavishly dressed window at the warm sunset that shimmered and slanted between the skyscrapers. Then, I climbed up into the four-poster bed and snuggled into smooth silk sheets.

I lay propped up but sinking into cushy pillows and sipped the Dom Pérignon Rosé my new agent had delivered with a crystal flute, my monogram etched in the side of the glass. I began to read the manuscript that had won me the admiration of some of today's most accomplished authors, now my peers, and I started to grow sleepy.

As I dozed off, the last thing I saw was the Swarvosky chandelier, glinting softly in its dimmed light, hovering like a crown for my rise to sudden, glorious fame.

I awoke to a horrible noise, a beeping like an alarm screaming the building was on fire. I cracked my eyes open to find the source of the incessant racket that was too close to my ear to be a building alarm.

On the nightstand, a small clock glowed 6:15 a.m. I swung my arm over my still sleeping head and slammed the snooze button. The only noise left was the grinding of school bus engines driving past the house and Dixie whining to be let out of her kennel.

The thick carpet my feet stepped up from when I climbed

into bed the night before had turned to cold hardwood. A robe—not the luxurious white one with *W.A.* embroidered on the lapel that I'd worn last night, but the faded blue one with stained pockets I'd gotten for Christmas two years ago—hung on the hook next to my bed.

I willed my stiff legs over the edge and creaked my way to upright. I grabbed the blue robe and shuffled to the kitchen to make coffee. Pouring a cup, I sat down to the scattered pages of yet another draft of my first novel that lay spread across my desk.

MBL Birch . *Creative Nonfiction*

Reflections on 2024
April 8, 2024, Texas Hill Country

We are in Texas for family matters, not for the eclipse. It's a few random minutes of darkness at mid-day, we think, but we are in the area, so why not? It's cloudy though, supposed to be cloudy all day, so pre-dawn finds us driving toward our best guess at open skies. We stop in a city park that the radar says will be only eighty percent clouds. Not great odds, but the best we can find. So, to fill the morning hours, we wander on foot, photographing unfamiliar birds and flowers. The park fills with eclipse seekers, to my dismay—I like solitude—but clearing skies are promising.

The moon begins to carve its path across the solar disk, so we return to our car: time for the paper eclipse glasses.

Cue the clouds.

Totality approaches. Clouds grow thicker and thicker, covering the sun entirely.

And then, at the moment that totality begins—as darkness falls, as a chill spreads through the air, as a group of confused vultures flies down across the river to roost—a small opening in the clouds appears, revealing the moon, and behind it, the sun.

Cheers of joy all around. Mine too, utterly unexpected—I am not the cheering type, after all.

Someone nearby has a violin. He's not a professional, but it is exactly right. Violin music, clouds shifting across the sky, cheers rippling across our momentary community each time the sun and moon are revealed.

And then it is done, the darkness lifts, the vultures return to their thermals in the sky. I am left to my musings on how community makes the magic happen, how the imperfect can be wondrous, and how the sun promises to come back out.

Sue Bruns . *Poetry*

Night Wind's Message

Outside the bedroom window
Wind's hand clasps a broken branch,
scratches sharp words, screeching notes—
replays hurtful phrases from old arguments,
etches messages on the pane.

Memory is merciless
when the wind stirs up dead leaves
and engraves broken promises
on the bedroom window.

Richard Fenton Sederstrom . *Poetry*

Sepia Weathers

That winter I had found my grandparents' old
Cocker Spaniel, Freckles, in the laundry room
lying curled around his empty food bowl. Freckles,
whom I had loved, and for whom I would grieve
f'rever'n'ever, had never enjoyed the company
of small boys. I would teach myself to pretend old.

Somewhere in an old album is a photo of Freckles.
An oval portrait. Sepia. It was taken years before
I was born to grow old, lying now curled round
the tinder-slash of sepia weathers, and now I can
stop the flow of another poem that is too long.
It's another failed poem, I know. Good: I *know.*

The holes. But sand will fill the holes. The sand
that subverts every hour fills every hole. Or ash
of FireWood. The aspen, jack pine, and red pine
refill scar-holes left from corporate ignitions, fill
the holes that greed has left for now, until the last
ghost has slipped into the final hole—left on some
depopulated Earth. Homes burned down to cellar
holes, mourned only by age-bowed orphan lilacs.

Susan Niemela Vollmer . *Poetry*

Fence

My neighbor built a fence
Tall and broad and dark
I no longer can see the purple phlox
Blooming behind the garage down the street
Or watch the golden leaves dropping from the maple
Swirl and puddle on the grass below
My neighbor built a fence

Still from my deck I watch Orion
Trail the crescent moon across the night sky
And on my neighbor's fence
A sunlit chickadee flits
Announcing its name for all to hear

Dawn Tanner . *Creative Nonfiction (Honorable Mention)*

Banshee Keening Prairie

The howling wind threatened to sweep inside the dorm apartment where I was staying and blow right through me. It had been wailing and shrieking for hours, making sleep impossible. It seemed to gain strength with the passing minutes. Curled up in bed, pensively listening, I wondered if I was brave enough to head into that wind on foot, in the dark, to a blind at the end of a prairie footpath.

I was visiting Crookston, which is surrounded by farmland, prairies, wetlands, and aspen forests. Although we have lost more than 99% of our prairies in Minnesota, there are many protected areas around Crookston. One of these is the Tympanuchus Wildlife Management Area (WMA), featuring 840 acres of tallgrass prairie. The name, *Tympanuchus*, is the genus for prairie chickens. These native prairie birds are especially interesting because of their springtime mating dance. The males gather to show off their best moves, while the females evaluate the dancers and choose the male that they like best.

What exactly are they looking for? I can't tell you, but I guess a female prairie chicken knows it when she sees it.

I was lucky to be visiting at the height of mating season, and Tympanuchus WMA has one of the best viewing blinds around. The blind, a simple canvas hut, is unique in the area because it's very close to the lekking ground so the view is spectacular. To avoid disturbing the prairie chickens, a walk in the dark is required to arrive before sunrise.

I had time that afternoon to drive by the roadside pull-off, so I would know where to start on the path that night. When I got back to campus, I packed a few essentials including a flashlight and a fleece blanket, prepped a thermos for steeping tea in the morning, and crawled into bed. That's when the wind found its fury, whistling through the crevasses of the eaves and making the building shudder.

It felt like an eternity, but finally, the alarm went off at

3:45 am. Time to go.

The wind buffeted the car as I drove through the nondescript dark. I arrived, parked, and, flashlight in hand, headed down the grassy path. At last, the wind seemed calmer.

When I arrived at the blind, I ducked under the door flap and scooted in. I silently slid a camp chair into position, dug into my bag to grab my camera, and tucked it next to my feet. Then I peeled open the canvas window flap, peered into the darkness . . . and waited.

I listened to the quiet of the prairie. The wind had finally ceased its constant moan. Silence fell heavy in its place. Slowly, the night sky shed its starry blanket, one little light extinguished at a time. The horizon began to glow with subtle pinks and purples.

I wondered how long I would need to wait.

Then, a shadow whirred past and landed, then another, and another. The prairie chickens were flying in low to take their positions, directly on the other side of that flimsy piece of canvas.

As the sun emerged above the horizon and rays lit up the prairie, the male prairie chickens burst into action, cooing, warbling, and keening as they stomped and challenged each other. I spotted the secretive females on the edges, furtively ducking and weaving through the crowd to get a closer look. The males inflated their bright orange throat pouches as they sang and even flew at each other.

The sun rose higher. At once, there appeared to be agreement that the show was over. With a whirring of wings, the prairie chickens flew off in every direction, disappearing into the golden ripples and waves of grasses.

The flurry and spectacle was all-consuming, but their wild orchestra was even better. I would say it was otherworldly—except that it was so stunningly this-worldly—and worthy of our awe, protection, and a future.

Tammy Tisdell . *Fiction*

Love At First Sight

Time froze in an instant when my eyes connected with his. The world around us disappeared when I saw him for the first time; our eyes locked.

Some might say I was drawn in by the beauty of his deep brown eyes with the shadow of thick black lashes, but it went far beyond that, I was taken to the depths of his soul. I knew in an instant that this was a love that would last forever, nothing would ever part us.

His name, Kaden, I had known that for a while.

I had known him by name but had never seen him in person, only photos. Now gazing at him face to face, I knew that my life would never be the same.

I fantasized about the time we would spend together. Picnics at the park, sporting events, snuggling up to watch movies together.

He was the type who would pick me wildflowers from the side of the road. I sensed the intensity of his love. I felt the beauty he saw in me, even though my hair was a mess, tangled in a bun on top of my head. I had put on make-up in the morning, but I could imagine that my lipstick was gone, and my mascara smeared, as I had just finished the most intense workout of my life. Kaden did not seem to notice or to care.

I had an impassioned mix of emotions. Exhausted, delighted, hopeful and a little scared. I could feel the presence in the room had become substantial; my life had changed in an instant. I proclaimed that one day I would meet Kaden, but I had not expected it to be today.

He had taken me by surprise, and I could sense that he would astonish and delight me for the rest of my life. We were both entranced as we gazed at each other affectionately, neither of us able to speak. We had a connection like I had never had with anyone, an unbreakable bond between a mother and her son.

Gail Lipe . *Poetry (Honorable Mention)*

Migraine

shooting stars announce its arrival
in my eyes
making it hard to see

the undulating zigzag aura
       catapults the stars
from one side
     to the other

as a nylon strap tightens
slowly around my head
suffocating thoughts
making
      memories
          impenetrable

pressure builds causing pain
around my skull
      behind my eye
a beating drum, a clashing cymbal

left out, my stomach
joins the chorus
nausea striking a chord
that rises to the pain

a symphony of torture
leaving my body weak with pain
I escape into sleep

Erin Lynn Marsh . *Poetry*

Postcard To My Dad in The Fall

Yesterday I took a photo of a tree, a smidge of orange
painting its leaves. In the fall, this tree is ablaze—

it is enough to remind you of Moses' burning bush.
When I pass by, I half expect it to speak. What

would it say? It has been watching the hummingbird
suspended in midair, a marionette parented

by the wind. I think it notices the days
getting shorter and I am grieving, already,

your death. The part of my heart that loves you—
is changing color, leaving me alone.

You will be dead and I will be tired.

You, who will not show me love.

Jayna Locke . *Poetry*

Implosion

It happens ever so slowly.
An implosion that lasts a lifetime.
First, each heart fissure deepens
Like the crags of the canyonlands,
Worn and shorn by wind and inland seas.

Then my mistakes become tumbleweeds
Blowing along the remote and dusty
Roadways of my mind,
Until they are caught and held forever
In the teeth of my cranium's barbed wire fences.

Add losses, for they too are plentiful,
Swirling incessantly through my life
Like a bathtub drain,
Taking the baby, the bath water, the kitchen sink.
All the things.

Yet I am an amalgam of wholeness
When the implosion is done.
Patched and stitched,
Mended by laughter and heart to hearts.
Held together by something greater than myself, I know
        not what.

Sue Bruns . *Creative Nonfiction*

The Frog Hunt

"Want to help me catch some frogs?"

Suzie jumps up and follows her brother to the hayfield.

Tom grabs Ma's lidded bucket and they set off across the farmyard, past the chicken coop to the freshly mown hayfield.

Their timing is right. Frogs spring from loose mats of moist hay, drying in the summer sun. Soon they'll be fishing bait for Mr. Hilger, Tom's seventh grade science teacher.

Suzie had found quarter-sized frogs and toads in Grandma's dirt-floored cellar, but the ones in the hayfield are lean, long-legged leopard frogs. She follows her big brother, high-stepping into the field, wading through the newly cut tangle. Frogs leap in all directions. Tom snatches one mid-jump and quickly drops it into the bucket. Suzie swipes at another but misses. She is afraid to pounce when they jump, so she stands and watches. Her brother times their leaps, anticipates where they'll land, swoops down with an open hand, snatches them, puts them into the bucket, and slaps the cover back on before they can escape.

Suzie tries again. The black-spotted frogs hide beneath the hay until she steps too close. Before long she isn't squeamish of their wriggling legs and long-toed feet, their moist bodies— twice the size of her hands.

The more frogs they catch, the more challenging the entrapment. Each time the lid is opened, there's risk of an escape. Within half an hour they have a half-filled bucket of kicking frogs, bumping against the lid and sides of the bucket.

"That's enough," Tom says. "Let's go."

He leads the way back to the farmyard, carrying the bucket by the handle. Suzie follows, ignoring the frogs they scare up along the way.

Ma is at the house, visiting with Grandma. Tom secures the lid and puts the bucket in the back seat of the car. They say goodbye to Grandma, and Ma drives back to town.

At Mr. Hilger's house, Tom grabs the frog pail out of the car.

"I need my bucket back," Ma reminds him.

Suzie follows her brother up the walk and he knocks on the door. Mrs. Hilger greets them, smiling. Her husband is not home, but she knows what's in the bucket and is ready with a few dollars.

"My ma needs her bucket back," Tom says.

"Oh," says Mrs. Hilger, and she goes to the laundry room for a scrub bucket.

As soon as Tom removes the lid, the twenty or so frogs that had settled into a relatively sedate tangle start to squirm, then jump—legs springing, feet clawing their way up their cohorts, attempting to escape. Three sets of hands cannot contain them. Thinking quickly, Tom tips the bucket to pour the frogs from Ma's bucket to Mrs. Hilger's.

There in the entryway near the open door to the basement and another door to the kitchen, the two children and Mrs. Hilger scramble for frogs, leaping in every direction. She stretches out her apron to block them from jumping down the stairs; Tom tries to channel them into the woman's pail as they spring to escape into the kitchen. Little Suzie chases one hopping frog across the kitchen floor toward the dining room while another frog slips under the refrigerator.

As the last frogs drop from Ma's bucket, Mrs. Hilger scurries about her kitchen, uttering desperate words to the frogs: "Oh! No, get back here! Into the pail. Not under there! Oh! Oh!"

She pushes the money into Tom's hand and thanks him. One frog follows the children out before the screen door slams shut. Tom carries Ma's bucket to the car.

As they drive off, Suzie can see Mrs. Hilger through her kitchen window, running about, scooping up frogs, and, likely, cursing her husband's bait order.

From the front seat, her brother hands Suzie a dollar, her share of the profits.

Rebecca Rae . *Creative Twist*

S'more With the Wind

The blistering wail of the siren broke the evening's otherwise serene silence. Graham crackers and chocolate bar pieces lay on a tray, like square customers in a patio massage parlor waiting to be slathered with hot, sticky marshmallows instead of wax.

Having been speared and lightly browned, most of our marshmallows had reached that perfect golden state of firepit bliss, except for my little brother Jonah's. He always waited until his resembled a briquette.

Dixie, still damp from our afternoon at the lake, jumped up, wagged her tail, and, after giving an obnoxious sand-sprinkling shake, yowled at the sound of the siren.

The weather was perfectly calm, so no one was too concerned right away. Then Mom said, "Sheesh, this still air is a stark comparison to the breeze we had earlier."

We lived on the edge of town so it was pretty dark right around us, but we could see the city's lights reflecting off the clouds in a pretty, iridescent orangish-yellow.

Fascinated by the chemical reaction of melting sugar, Jonah hardly noticed the siren blaring or Dad's words that followed. His eyes and mind were busy intently studying his now burning marshmallow. "I don't feel right about this weather. It's *too* still. Maybe we should head inside to the basement," Dad said, looking unsure but not uncalm.

I elbowed my brother. "Hullooow! Didn't you hear? We're going inside."

Shook from his reverie, Jonah whined, "Aw, we were just getting started! Maybe they're just doing one of those emergency system tests."

"You're a dork," I said. "They only do that on Wednesdays during the day. It's Saturday night in case you didn't notice."

Like the powerful rotor wash from a rapidly descending helicopter that suddenly appeared over our patio, the red and white checkered tablecloth Mom had laid out on the table was whipped up and blown away by a gust of wind, taking the s'more fixings with it.

Dad caught the lantern just before it crashed onto the patio stones. "All right, that's it. Everybody inside," he said as he bounded towards the bucket of water we always kept near the fire.

"No, Dad! Let's go storm chasing! C'mon, we did it last summer, remember? Even Dixie came with!"

"Jonah, we did that during the day. It's too dark this time. We won't see anything anyway," Mom said, trying to appease him even though she wanted to go too. Mom and Jonah were the risk-takers of the family.

"Can I finish my s'more first?" My little brother had no sooner asked than another gust of wind blasting painful hail pellets blew it out of his hand.

We heard the patio table umbrella ripped from its pole and saw it fly overhead as we all raced across the yard toward the house. The rain came so fast and hard we could hardly see. We made a chain, grabbing onto each other so we wouldn't get confused on which way to go.

Dripping wet and stinging from pelting rain and ice stones, we made it into the dark house just before we heard an eardrum-shattering "crack" followed by a thunderous boom we all felt.

We made it safely to the basement but didn't need to stay long. The storm was strong but left as quickly as it hit. The next morning was sunny, and the birds sang "good morning" as my family went outside to look over any damage.

---

lantern, iridescent, stark, damp, coincidence, broken, blistering, bound.

Tammy Tisdell . *Fiction (Honorable Mention)*

The Choice

Eve welcomed the pain that overtook the numbness that had entrapped her for the past three weeks. The sting of the frigid wind made her face hurt. The snow crunched beneath her with every difficult step as she staggered across the yard to the field behind the house. The trail of red droplets from her own, self-inflicted wounds on her wrists contrasted with the white blanket that covered the earth.

Everything slipped into slow motion; Eve struggled to the spot where Abby had been found. She longed for her lifeblood to mix with her daughter's again, as it had when she carried Abby in her womb.

The perfectionist in Eve cringed as she saw the bloodline that she had left behind. Why hadn't she waited to bring death upon herself until she was on the hallowed ground where Abby's life had been taken.

Eve had left the house meticulous. Deep down she knew that she would give in to this evil. Organized to her core, she washed her husband's work clothes. Then mindlessly she made a homemade pie. She scoured the bathroom and scrubbed the floors while it baked. The scent of cinnamon and apples overtook her as she finished cleaning the kitchen. She turned off the oven and placed the overstuffed pie on the counter where Abby used to sit when eating her favorite dessert.

Everything was perfect, except Eve herself. She glanced at the clock on her phone one last time. If Adam walked through the door on time, he would stop her from this grave sin.

Instead, she saw his text.

Working late, eat without me.

She let her breath out slowly. It was time. She blamed Adam for not being there. Everything would be different if he were there to protect her from herself.

Eve shivered. Her breath went before her, imitating puffs of smoke. She was almost to the edge of the field. The last few steps felt like an eternity. Now at the tree she hugged it, ready to embrace death itself.

Wiping her nose on her sleeve, she turned and slid to the ground. She scraped her back as her sweater pulled up around her waist, leaving her bare skin uncovered. She had not bothered with a jacket.

Eve loved her husband and son, but could no longer go on without her daughter, her very breath. Her son Cain would be able to make his way without her; he was mostly grown and would have his father.

She dug in her pocket to pull out the handful of aspirin. She knew that slitting her wrist would be a slow death and wanted to thin her blood so the hopelessness would be sure to end.

At that moment, she heard a bird; turning to the side, she saw a dove had landed. The moment was fleeting, and it flew away chirping. Eve was perplexed as she realized there was something in the snow near the spot she was staring at.

Leaning over, she reached out and pulled a brown leather journal from the snowbank. She flipped it open and realized it was void of word.

Without thinking she wiped a spot of blood that she had dripped on it. The blood smeared over the page revealing words.

God help me. I didn't mean to kill her.

Energy drained from her body, Eve immediately called her husband on speakerphone. She tucked the journal in her waistband, then pressed both wrists against her jeans, to slow the bleeding as she waited for Adam.

Later Eve awoke to someone poking her with a needle. Taking in the rails on the side of the bed and the bag of liquid hanging over her head, she realized it was a nurse inserting an IV.

Her husband was across the room talking with a man in dark blue scrubs. The doctor was telling him, "She is going to be just fine; good thing you got there when you did."

Eve let her eyes flutter shut until the medical staff had left the room. Adam pulled the chair close to her bed and took her hand. He jumped when Eve opened her eyes and said softly in desperation, "Where is the journal?"

Adam looked confused.

"The Brown Leather Journal, where is it?"

"I tossed it in the backseat when I brought you here."

"Get it."

"Honey . . . "

"Now."

Adam did not want to push her over the edge; she seemed crazed. He went to retrieve the journal.

When he got to the car, he flipped open the journal. It was blank. He fanned the pages and saw red. He realized there was a blood stain that snaked down the page revealing words.

He tucked it securely under his jacket and headed to the gift shop. He had to find the coloring book with the magic pen that revealed invisible ink.

Back in the hospital room, he looked at Eve and, without saying a word, handed her the journal and the magic pen. Together they scribbled fiercely.

On the third page they saw his name, the one who had destroyed their family. They looked at each other and began to cry. The pain cut deeper than anyone could imagine. They had a decision to make: do they turn him over to the police or do they protect the only child they have left?

Charmaine Pappas Donovan . *Poetry*

Return of a Bad Dream

An ominous feeling, dreadful really,
how he struck with cruel finality—
faulted me for five days of making our trip fall flat—

But is it really that, or a line drawn somewhere
between us like an invisible boundary
in that space which separates us as we sleep?

Perhaps time has eroded our friendship,
which now requires more effort to maintain,
which most things do as part of the aging process.

Sometimes I think he is a stranger,
someone I thought I knew, but really don't
have a clue as to his true identity.

Could that be the source of my fear?
Or do my imaginings run away with me,
yanking me back to a place I hate to revisit?

James Walsh . *Poetry*

Polar Vortex

Nothing moves on the street today

No dog walkers, no joggers
no leg-stretchers. No scurry
of squirrels, no twitter of bird call

All is still—not even a car in motion,
oil like sludge, fuel lines and batteries
taxed to their lower limits.

Bitter tongues of crystalline miasma
probe the lap siding, the poor insulation,
the rattled windows and doors, for the
slightest point of entry

Searching for a thermal host,
to gnaw at souls kept barely warm
by tepid thoughts of an uncertain spring.

Charmaine Pappas Donovan . *Poetry (Honorable Mention)*

If Flowers Forgive
Words cannot forgive.
Only hearts and flowers can.

Can I find forgiveness hidden under a rock?
Do flowers forgive wind for stealing their petals?
Is forgiveness a forgotten place, hazy and remote,
a road overgrown and unrecognizable?
Directions are gone: a map lost or thrown away.

Where do I find forgiveness?
I say the words. They are empty.
He took my legs, my teenage years, my friends.
Is twenty-five years long enough for him to pay?
I live a lifetime in a wheelchair,
I said the words, *I forgive you.*
But does the girl within forgive?
The one shot by her fourteen-year-old classmate.
He killed three friends in our prayer group.
Let his life behind bars be enough,
like my life in a wheelchair must be enough.
Let his bullets be the parole board's decision:
still a black mark at the end of his sentence.

I sigh with a relief I do not feel
like legs that cannot move or carry me.
He won't go free. The parole verdict is final.
He hears voices; he is still a present danger.
I beg my heart to carry me to that forgotten place
where tears fall like rain on thirsty fields.
I will let wind whisk away the girl who lost her legs.
I will learn to forgive like a plucked flower.

Mike Lein . *Creative Twist*

Degrees of Difficulty

People living in the warm climates of Iowa and Wisconsin often seem amazed that I can survive bitter cold in the Northwoods. Especially on extended visits to my cabin with only a woodstove for heat and an outhouse for sanitary facilities. I've got two words for those nice people—"preparation and planning." Things I've refined over thirty years of cabin life.

"Cold" means different things to different people. I've been to Arizona for winter vacations where temperatures have sunk into the forties. Residents shuffle around dressed in puffy coats, stocking hats, and shorts. They claim its "cold"—"Arizona Cold" since they've survived blistering heat in an "Arizona Hot" summer.

Let's start with thirty-two degrees as "Northwoods Cold." That's when ice forms on lakes, rivers and, coincidently, on hands and other exposed body parts. Life at the cabin is easy. It's hard to keep the woodstove dialed back to less than eighty inside. A light pair of long underwear (longies) under jeans, a flannel shirt and an insulated vest are needed for outdoor trips. Any more clothes cause me to break out in a damp sweat while hauling firewood. The trip to the outhouse is a leisurely stroll even if the winter darkness requires a lantern to light the way.

Outdoor life gets complicated around fifteen degrees. Thicker longies and a light jacket over an insulated vest are needed for hauling firewood, removing the dock from the frozen lake (should have done that last month), or taking the dogs on their twentieth driveway walk of the day. A trip to the outhouse can be made without bundling up if you're quick. The insulated toilet seat is a real game changer here. A local artist made mine out of inch-thick pink foam insulation glued to sturdy plywood, cut in the classic shape.

Zero degrees. Life gets difficult but not impossible. Northwoods men and women have a saying—"There is no bad weather—only bad clothing."

My office wall includes a picture of Minnesota adventurer Will Steger having a picnic with his fellow travelers and dog team. They're relaxing in iridescent snow suits that contrast with the starkly cold white ice and snow of Antarctica. They didn't buy their trekking clothes at Walmart. But that's an extreme case. Cost-effective cold weather clothes will allow outdoor fun at zero degrees. Just layer on more layers depending on how low the price was, and temperature is.

I get by with mid-weight longies, fleece-lined pants, insulated hoodie, vest and coat. I can haul firewood and walk the dogs with ease in the sheltered cabin yard. The trip to the outhouse does get complicated. The upper layers resist movement in the tight confines of the little building. Layers must be unbound. Then layers must be relayered in correct order when the task is complete. And thank the Northwoods gods for the insulated toilet seat!

Work below minus fifteen becomes tough, real tough. Firewood must be hauled. Larger quantities need to be stockpiled inside to keep the stove roaring. Other activities aren't worth the time and effort to dress. The dash to the outhouse must happen, encumbered by layers, clunky boots, AND a pair of insulated coveralls entombing the layers. As few layers as possible are unlayered to accomplish what's needed.

Fifteen below is my personal limit for extended outdoor activity. I have hunted, ice-fished and hiked at worse temperatures in the past. Now I've made lifestyle changes that don't require much other than the firewood and outhouse stuff. I'm thankful for the simplicity of the woodstove and the outhouse with the insulated seat. People with running water and indoor outhouses are dealing with broken water pipes, furnaces dying at midnight, and septic tanks frozen into underground blocks of stinky ice. I remain inside, fully stocked with firewood, the stove blazing away, very carefully preparing and planning for the next trip to the outhouse.

lantern, iridescent, stark, damp, coincidence, broken, blistering, bound.

MBL Birch . *Creative Nonfiction*

Water and Stone

If magma stirs beneath the surface of the earth, but there is no one to see it, does it glow?

The heat swells from below. Solid rock flows upward like thick caramel, over time measured in the lifespans of gods. In this place, water is not water, but something else, something like—and unlike—water.

Above, molten rock strains against the brittle skin of the earth until the land splits open, violent and magnificent. Steam fills the air as lava spills from the wounded earth, flowing across her surface, layer upon layer upon layer.

Each morning, the sun casts light across the harsh landscape. There are no witnesses.

A million mornings dawn. Then eight thousand million more.

The earth ceases to bleed.

Waters overtake the land, and new life arises, life that does not mark the days, the years, the eons, except by its living and dying.

Time passes.

Ice spreads from the north as winter sets in. Somewhere, far away, primates are learning to control fire, but here, in this place, there is only the ice, and beneath it, the earth.

The long winter comes to a close, and ice turns to water.

Superior has many voices. Today, the great water is whispering: its waves caress the edges of the pebble beach. My child is not whispering: he is singing as he runs across the shore, his feet kicking up smooth stones along the way. At the edge of the water, he comes to a halt, gestures dramatically as if summoning a spirit, then turns and retreats at full speed. It makes me laugh aloud. He, too, is laughing. He crouches down and picks up one of the uncountable stones—dark and flat, it fits in the palm of his hand.

"Basalt," I tell him. "It's very old."

He turns to face the lake, positions himself carefully, and flings the stone across the surface of the water. Then he spins back, jubilation on his face, his arms wide open to the sky: "Five skips!"

Marlys Guimaraes . *Poetry*

Pull of the Portal

The photo, a sunlit trail leading into the forest
below a canopy of brilliant fall-flamed maples

See how it beckons

like a child entering a snow tunnel
or door to tented blankets in the living room

Observe an oval opening in granite boulders
announcing an undiscovered cave

Feel how its mystery summons—

Who can resist the urge to enter an arched
garden gate with a winding floral path

I contemplate life's final door, wondering
how it will lure me onto its loving path

knowing, like all portals, it must be explored,
a long, crooked finger that whispers—*come in*

Lorie Yourd . *Poetry*

Storing Sugar

It has been two years . . . the sugar is gone. I don't cook or bake like you did, but hummingbird food requires a half-cup in a four to one ratio. I wash the empty bin gently to preserve the label written in your hand.

Unfolding a stepstool to fetch more from the pantry you built, I sense your presence, arm stretched overhead, retrieving what we need from the highest shelf.

The pink and white sugar sack has been taped shut and pressed into a gallon Ziploc hallowed by your touch. With effort, I peel away the plastic and loosen the seal—your meticulous care.

Sugar in water, simple syrup poured into a glass globe—I cling to thoughts of other summers, the flurries of colorful feathers, our shared rituals.

Pamela Wolters . *Poetry*

Lakeshore Time

Time loses its way upon reaching the lake.
Father Sun ambles on his circuitous journey,
indolent as a bee drunk on pollen.
Faces and arms acquire a bronze glow,
patina of Summer's bliss.
Lapping waves provide the soundtrack,
echoes of life in the slow lane.
Embedded in purified sand,
bare footprints dissolve in minutes,
deleted like obsolete texts.
Polished pebbles resemble pearls of great price.
Salvaged driftwood transforms into memorabilia.

Laws of lake shore time
call for loosening care's iron grip.
Wrist watches are consigned to home,
schedules to wastebaskets,
decluttering minds at the call of a loon.
Supper is delayed until hunger
raises its voice. Star-studded skies
percolate wisdom filtered through a breeze,
inviting all to drink deeply
of the cup of peace.

Chris Marcotte . *Creative Nonfiction*

It's What Moms Do

We fly across the street like ribbon tails on a kite. I am afraid, and Mom is terrified. In one hand, she has the handle of the wagon, with the little kids inside. In the other hand, she has my sister's small hand. My brother holds our sister's hand and I, the oldest, hold tight to him. On the other side of the street. Mom stops to make sure that we are all right and that we still have our books. We are on our way to the library. What a challenge for Mom, with five children between the ages of seven and one, to make the trek every week or two.

The first part of our walk is the most difficult. It is uphill and then across Seventh Avenue. Next, we cross the four sets of railroad tracks where the little kids giggle, and my brother always looks for smashed pennies. After climbing another hill, we turn onto wide streets named after presidents with old houses, huge trees, and very little traffic.

This is where my heart soars, and I know Mom relaxes some as well. Fall is the very best. We crunch and shuffle through the burgundy, rust, and yellow leaves of the oaks, maples, and elms. Even if I sometimes must hold hands with my siblings, I feel a sense of intense happiness—a chance to skip and twirl and sing—abandoned elation that Dad would never allow.

By the time we arrive at the library, every one of us is ready for the bathroom and the drinking fountain. The wagon is left outside, and Mom carries the little kids while we hold the doors open. After we return our books, my sister, brother, and I head for the children's area. We each get to pick two or three books to take home.

Mom spreads a small blanket on the floor near the grown-up books and sets the little kids on it. She scans titles in the nonfiction section and quickly makes her selection before something happens. At times Mom must feel like a cartoon character with us tugging on her arms or legs, seeking her attention, or needing her to settle a squabble. I wonder if she ever comes home with a book she grabbed by mistake in her attempt to keep one of the little kids from getting away.

Our time in the library is short, much shorter than the walk. With a wave, we are out the door. I carry my books possessively in the cloth bag Mom had made; the straps cross my chest and go over one shoulder. Mom makes denim bags for everything. When we pack for the cabin, we use our denim duffle bag for our clothes. The outside pocket has room for our toothbrush and a small toy or book. For school we each have a denim bag for our lunch that has a pocket for our milk money.

Mom sews, cooks, cleans, and tries her hardest to keep a safe distance between us kids and our dad. He expects near perfection from us in manners, cleanliness, and behavior. Mom smiles, teaches us songs, and never lets us see her cry.

Three blocks from home, we make another death-defying race across Seventh Avenue and Mom might mutter a prayer. By then, we are tired and cranky. We may stop at Pearl's Dairy for a treat to share. Or Mom hurries us along because she still has something that needs to be done before our dad gets home. About a block from the house Mom looks for his car; if it isn't there, she grins.

Half a dozen years later, we ride our bikes to the library. Mom doesn't look for Dad's car anymore. And she walks to Seventh Avenue every morning to catch the bus to her classes at the University of Minnesota.

Jan Chronister . *Creative Twist*

Blue Moon

Still damp plate
slips from my hands,
hits the sink with a sound
too stark for hope.
By lucky coincidence
it breaks perfectly,
each piece an iridescent
half moon.

Memories blister my mind.
It was my mother's wedding china,
blue Luray from 1943.

I console myself,
consider the broken remnants
bound for garden art,
planted where they will glow
with reflected lantern light.

*lantern, iridescent, stark, damp, coincidence, broken, blistering, bound.

Linda Maki . *Poetry*

My Grandmother was Born in 1900

Lately, I've been thinking of how
she would have been twenty in 1920.
Was she a flapper? Did she Charleston?
I don't know. I never asked.

In the depression thirties was her little
family destitute? Did Grandpa lose
his job? Stand in bread lines?
I don't know. I never asked.

In the forties was she a Rosie
the Riveter? Use ration coupons?
Plant a Victory Garden?
I don't know. I never asked.

Life flowed long for her.
Wars, pandemics, great inventions?
Which ones shaped her existence?
I wish I would have asked.

Bernadette Hondl Thomasy . *Poetry*

One Day

If you think life is short,
consider the daylily
Just twelve hours in bloom

Anchored to the earth
on a stem of green,
star petals unfurled
the daylily gives beauty and
pleasure to the world
for a single day

Like the lily
each of us exists
but a nanosecond
in eternity

one life
one lily
one day

Norita Dittberner-Jax . *Poetry*

Self-Portrait

The outer woman, pale,
skinned of hair by the latest
hairdresser, carries January's
poundage like her schoolbag,
the same burden every day.
Very little changes—teacher,
wife, mother, friend. She breaks
out of herself as she can.

The inner woman is no woman
but a girl, flushed and leggy,
loving the wind, running into it,
on the threshold of everything.

Let something of the girl remain
always with the pale face. Let them
rest in another like nesting dolls.
The girl, her most true self,
wanting it all to happen. Now.

Jeanne Everhart . *Creative Nonfiction*

Wilderness Spirit Hunting

This morning I can see my breath in the tent. My warm sleeping bag is difficult to leave and I dress inside downy confines. After breakfast there is no urge or reason to linger in camp. We are here to put meat in our freezer for winter.

My husband Doug and I walk across the shallow river channel and into the thick brush. A shrubbery pathway we call "the tunnel" leads to a slough. We have named river channels that have become familiar—Wolf Run, Porcupine Crossing, Tall Pines, and Cranberry. Crisp breaths of air clear my head. Alders are turning gold, cranberries are ripe, wild rose bush leaves and hips of red reflect on the water. I sample a rose hip.

We part company and will meet back here at the end of day. I hike through the woods as Doug crosses the slough in his hip boots through mud that mires you if you hesitate. There are tracks of a cow and calf moose, and a large bear paw print. A hawk calls overhead while flying from view.

The river is high this year. Strolling beside a flooded river channel, I pause when a big black bear suddenly appears on the opposite bank a short way ahead of me. The bear is looking across the river. I make myself known, stepping from the trees and chamber a round in my rifle. The breeze is favorable to the bear so he has to know I am here. "Stay on that side of the river," I tell him.

Surprising me, the bruin wades into the river and begins swimming across. I am in awe of the beautiful black coat and the size of this magnificent animal swimming with ease. My heart is pounding.

"Just go on your way, bear—I don't want to shoot you!"

I watch breathless, hoping he doesn't approach me coming out of the water. If I shoot the loud noise would discourage any moose in the area, and if the bear is wounded or it falls into the river that will not be good. My finger releases the safety on my rifle.

Reaching shore the bear pauses to shake off water like a dog, then fortunately goes into the woods away from me. Not wanting to collide head-on in the woods, I too turn around and backtrack with an unforgettable memory.

A big animal crashes through the dense brush—I pause and listen. Whatever was startled is not going to show itself. I remove my backpack, find a spot to sit and watch where tracks in the silt show activity of animals coming to drink. I hear the current of the river's main channel rippling and churning.

An occasional breeze rustling through leaves punctuates wilderness silence. The buzz of mosquitoes is magnified. Chickadees flit about me calling to one another in song and chitter. It's so quiet I can hear the flutter of their wings. Red squirrels chatter and declare territory in their quest to gather pine cones and mushrooms to cache for winter. A tiny weasel, dashing in and out of a pile of driftwood, studies me for a second, then darts away.

A porcupine waddles out of the woods. I become a statue observing him as he observes me momentarily, then walks to the water's edge and drinks. Were it not for those quills, I would reach out and pet him. He gives me a sideways glance and disappears back into the trees.

Hunting makes me very aware of my remote surroundings and the inhabitants. Senses sharpened, I am conscious of every twig snap and every pebble disturbed. Hunting gives me time to sit silently, absorb nature, and listen in introspective thought as my spirit is renewed in this "real world."

Constance Neumiller . *Poetry*

Beads of Rain

We are two
Beads of rain

Falling to earth
Facing our fate

Colliding with dirt
Losing our shape

Forgiving ourselves
Dissolving our pain

Audrey Kletscher Helbling . *Poetry*

Where There's Smoke, There's Fire

Smoke billows behind the garage,
a white cloud enveloping the backyard
with its ramshackle shed hauled in
last March on a beat-up pickup truck.

If trouble rides in on the wind,
then trouble arrives here on foot,
on bicycles, in cars and trucks.
Too many to count, at all hours.

Men sporting tattooed necks
and hoodies and pants that sag,
not the nice-to-meet-you neighborly type
who settle in and mind their own business.

Rather, their business happens swiftly,
often after dark, under the watchful eye
of a security camera that blinks purple,
surveilling arrivals and departures.

Sometimes they congregate, start a fire.
Smoke rises like a message to the gods.
Sparks fly, threatening to set the shack ablaze
while The Shed Guys smoke. And I watch.

Niomi Rohn Phillips . *Creative Twist*

Midwife on the Prairie

Margaretha heard the sobs, but the room was so dark, all she could see was a form huddled under a grungy sheet over a layer of straw on a board attached to the wall of the soddy. She pulled the sheet away and put a comforting hand on the young woman's forehead.

"It will be okay," she said, though she had no idea if the woman understood.

Her husband spoke a mixture of Yiddish, German, and English according to Abe, who had met Michael Gershman at Shepherd's Mercantile in town. The man was frantic, inquiring about a doctor, because his wife Rachel had been in labor all night. It was coincidental that he'd encountered Abe. "The doctor is a day's drive, but *mein frau* is a midwife," Abe told him.

By the time Abe got home to fetch Margaretha though, he'd had second thoughts. "They're Jews," he said.

"*Jah*, and they need me." Margaretha tied a scarf around her head and picked up her black bag from the bench by the door. "The Lord didn't bless me with this gift to deliver only Mennonite babies."

"We're bound not to associate with them though. If Reverend Doerksen hears of it . . ."

"Get the wagon, or I'll go by myself."

Michael Gershman had heard the horses and met them at the door. "*Kumm.*" He motioned them inside.

A black-shawled, scowling woman sat on a bench at a table, the only furniture in the room. Abe took his hat off and sat down across from her. Michael picked up a lantern and ushered Margaretha into the second room.

"Rachel." He nodded at the bed.

A rag covered the small window. Margaretha yanked it off, and the noonday sun beamed a ray of iridescent light into the stark, barren room.

"My mother-in-law covers the windows so demons can't get in and steal the baby." Rachel sobbed.

"There's no such thing as demons who steal babies." Margaretha gritted her teeth. "Only old women believe in such nonsense."

Rachel had been in labor for hours, now too weak to push when her body was ready. Margaretha coached her, "Breathe. Push. Breathe. Push." This was taking too long. "I will help you turn on your side. Changing your position will help."

Finally, the head emerged, but then, no more. Something was wrong.

Margaretha eased her hand into the vagina next to the tiny head and freed the shoulder.

"One more push, Rachel."

A scrawny boy emerged and, thankfully, cried out when Margaretha patted his back. She took a scissors from her bag, cut the cord, wrapped him in the clean blanket she always carried, and put him on his mother's chest.

She went to the door. "You have a son, Michael."

"*A dank, sheynem dank* (thank you, thank you very much)." Michael went to his wife and baby, Margaretha gathered her bag, Abe put his hat on, and they left.

"I thought you would want to stay," Abe said. "You usually stay a few hours."

"*Nein*. I've never been in such a damp, dreadful place, Abe. Or seen anyone so poor. They haven't had meat in months. Nor milk. Why are they near starving? The woods are full of animals. Don't they hunt? Didn't they have a garden?"

"They're city people. Not farmers. Never lived in the country. They were recruited to Homestead by some organization that convinced them they'd find less prejudice in the country."

A week later, Margaretha was gazing out the window when she saw Reverend Doerksen's buggy come up the driveway. She untied her apron, brushed away the hair escaping from her braid, and went to the door.

"Reverend Doerksen, welcome. What brings you out here

so early in the morning?"

"Is Abe home?"

"In the barn. I'll get him," she said, puzzled.

Abe greeted the minister and ushered him into the house. Doerksen declined the offer to sit down for coffee and launched immediately into his blistering pronouncement.

"It's come to my attention that you have been with the Jews." He paused and glared at them. "Infidels. You broke your vows. I expect you to confess your sin at Sunday services."

"I delivered their baby." Margaretha couldn't contain her contempt.

"The Bible is clear. I will see you Sunday morning." Doerksen turned and left.

"There's no sin in what I did. I will not confess." Margaretha's voice shook.

"We will be Shunned," Abe said. "We will sit alone at church gatherings, isolated from our community. My brother and his family won't be allowed to be with us. Swallow your pride, Margaretha."

Abe held her trembling hand at the front of the church. She refused to speak. He confessed for both of them. They weren't Shunned, but they were Shamed, and the shaming hung on like the winter cold. Women she'd helped give birth and men whose wives and babies she'd saved, turned their heads when she passed.

She was planting her garden when an ox cart came up the driveway. Michael Gershman jumped down from the wagon.

"You're leaving?"

"Yes, going to Chicago. Farming isn't for us. We came to say good-bye and *dank. Sheynem dank* for helping my Rachel. Saving our baby. God bless you for your kindness."

Margaretha gripped the hoe, crashed it into the ground. Clumps flew. What irony. She is blessed by the infidels' God, shamed by her Mennonite Jesus.

lantern, iridescent, stark, damp, coincidence, broken, blistering, bound.

Vicky A. King . *Poetry*

The Future

Against loud flowers of wallpaper,
the casket sat at the far end
of the long room
Alone
Cold
Her face expressionless and gray
Inviting no one.

With bruises like tattoos
afloat under their sheer skin,
classmates huddled in circle
like a secret society
Shadows staining faces,
half-drained of life's color
Lips thin and taut
Gossip pooled around their feet.
Eyes dart toward her box—
briefly
Not daring to look too long
lest they lose their own way
home.

Chris Marcotte . *Creative Twist*

Last Laugh

My brother Norman decided he was too old for Halloween when he finished eighth grade and worked with our dad. But I looked forward to the last days of October in our one-room country school. It was 1930, and, like any other holiday, it was celebrated with a program at school. This year our teacher encouraged us to dress up like the characters in the picture books on our library shelf.

Our parents and others in the community loved any excuse to gather, and Halloween was the first event since the fall term had begun. Besides the families, it was no coincidence that the bachelors from miles around were bound to attend as it gave them a chance to meet the "new teacher" who could become someone's "new Missus."

In the days leading up to the celebration, the younger kids were decorating the school with carefully scissored and pasted jack-o-lanterns, ghosts, black cats, and witches. We older kids were memorizing poems and songs. Our mothers helped us turn old clothes and bed sheets into costumes to resemble Humpty-Dumpty, Old King Cole, Cinderella, Mother Hubbard, and Santa Claus.

Two days before Halloween, I spied on Norman and his friend Eddie who were near the barn when I went to gather eggs.

"Let's go to Lofgren's house first," Norman said. He used a stick to draw an X in the dirt. "Then we can run across the field and get to the Jones's." Norman marked the route.

Eddie nodded. "He'll for sure be at the school—cuz of Glooriia," he added in a sing-song voice.

Norman's face reddened and he swatted Eddie. "We got time for one more. Who else's privy should we tip over?"

The dogs started to bark, and I didn't want them to give me away. I scurried back to the house with six eggs in my apron and slumped on the porch to catch my breath and to make sure I hadn't broken any. So, it's true, my brother *does* want to court the prettiest girl at school, too. And he wants to embarrass Ollie Jones who *was* courting her.

Ollie was funny, polite, and had gone on to attend the high school in town. I liked him, and didn't like it that my brother had mischievous plans. I told Gloria about the outhouse prank the next day during recess.

On Halloween our teacher had us practice our part for the evening program, and after lunch she excused us to go home and finish our costumes. Gloria and I left the school together. She told me that Ollie had a plan, though she didn't know what it was.

After supper, Mom helped me dress like an old lady because I am to recite all eight verses of "There was an Old Woman who Swallowed a Fly." Dad hitched the team to the hay wagon, and, after chores were done, he loaded a couple hay bales for us to sit on, a basket of Mom's fresh doughnuts, and a few lanterns for our trip home in the dark.

I sat on a bench next to the other fifth and sixth graders and watched the parents and community members arrive. When Ollie walked in, he caught my eye, nodded his head slightly, and winked. I felt the color creep up on my cheeks and turned to the front. If only I were a little older.

Most of the evening was a blur, but I was proud since I made just one mistake, and no one noticed. After the school part of the program was done, and the little kids were back near their parents, the lights were dimmed. A few candles cast an iridescent glow and made distorted shadows on the walls. One of the old timers recited "The Midnight Ride of Paul Revere," and another struck terror in some with his re-telling of "The Tell-Tale Heart."

The sky was pitch-dark as we left the schoolhouse. We were almost home when the wind picked up and with the whirling leaves came the awful stench of a neglected outhouse. "Pee-yew," we all said, covering our noses and gagging. Even our horses veered away from the smell.

"Pa," Norman called out from the ditch. "It's me and a couple other guys. Can we have a ride?"

"Are you boys what stinks?"

"Yeah, I guess we got a little damp. We fell in a privy hole."

Dad guffawed. "Not with the tomfoolery you've been up to. You boys get yourselves cleaned up in the pond before you even think of coming near the house."

"It's gonna be freezing in the water," Norman said.

"Yep," Dad said. "My guess is your privy-tipping has come to an end though."

My parents spoke of various punishments. I figured Norman was bound to get a real blistering.

I was in bed when Norman finally entered the kitchen. I heard him drag a chair close to the cookstove. Dad asked him who had moved the privy prior to the anticipated shenanigans.

"Ollie Jones," he said as his teeth chattered.

I laughed into my pillow. I now understood why Ollie had winked at me.

---

lantern, iridescent, stark, damp, coincidence, broken, blistering, bound.

Deborah Rasmussen . *Poetry*

Plant Sitter
for MK

What's her name? you ask
as I hand my Christmas Cactus
over to your care. I hadn't
thought of that. Somehow
you sense a soul
within the greenery—
which makes a name
imperative. How else
will you converse
while I'm away? How

do I converse
with an unnamed being
from whom I demand
annual blooms
whether or not
I remember to water,
prune, turn soil

now and then,
repot as needed,
be the carer
I ask you to be
these next weeks
because your plants

look so happy.
Her name is Chris, I reply,
as though I always knew it,
and she glows a little
          greener
when I say goodbye,
leave her in what I know
          to be
good hands.

Kara Tollerud . *Creative Twist*

The Book Retrieval

They took turns passing the lantern between them as they walked quietly down the damp, dark hallway.

Was it a coincidence they were here? Perhaps, they were bound to secrecy. Now, they had to finish their mission.

As they neared the end of the hallway, a door appeared in front of them.

This must be the right spot, they agreed.

The man opened the door cautiously. The doorknob wasn't broken. He followed the woman through the door.

The room was the opposite of the hallway. While the hallway was dark, the room had an iridescent glow to it.

The room was not stark. It was dancing with colors.

The atmosphere was inviting to the man and woman, but they knew they had to leave after completing their mission.

There along the wall under the window was a book shelf. The man and woman started reading through the titles.

"I've got it," the woman exclaimed.

She read the title to the man. *"Talking Stick 21, Nightfall."*

After basking in the dazzling room for a few more minutes, the man and woman departed.

He held the lantern while she held the book. They retraced their steps through the damp, dark hallway.

Once outside, nightfall had come upon them as the subtitle suggested. They didn't have to worry about getting burned by the blistering heat from the sun.

The woman relinquished control of the book to the college student who planned to study it and learn the feel of the contest.

What adventure would the man and woman embark on next?

*lantern, iridescent, stark, damp, coincidence, broken, blistering, bound.

Laura L. Hansen . *Poetry*

Caesura for Bernhart

Somewhere in the music
there is the sound of a triangle,
a single ting,

exquisitely timed, then a slow
swell like a sea wave rising,
a brush of metal

against steel, a cymbal barely
touched, then the breathy voice
of an oboe,

a distant seabird. Somewhere
in the music there is warm sand,
there is salt.

Somewhere in the music
there is you running with the dog,
seafoam and wrack,

gulls scattering at your approach.
Somewhere in the distance
there are violins,

there is a crescendo of waves,
a ship lost at sea, a caesura.
Where have you gone?

Alice Springer Marks . *Creative Twist*

Where Were You When the Lights Went Out?

When I was a little kid we used to sing a call and response ditty on the playground: "Where were you when the lights went out?" answered by "Down in the cellar eating sauerkraut." I'm not a little kid now, I'm not in the cellar, and I wouldn't eat sauerkraut if you paid me. The only coincidence is the power just went out at my uncle and aunt's farm.

I'm sixteen and staying here during summer vacation to help out while Auntie is in the hospital. I was gathering eggs when all went dark. I saw a flickering light in the barn and felt my way over there. Randy, the hired hand, good-looking dude, but with terrible grammar, had grabbed a battery-operated lantern from its usual hook and with its light was fiddling with the fuse box. He saw me and said, "It ain't fuses so must be a broke wire or somethin'." He paused a minute and said, "There's a nest of kittens in the hayloft. Do you wanna see them?"

Wary, I said, "Isn't it too dark to see them?"

"Duh. This here lantern will light our way."

I really didn't believe there were kittens, but I played along even though he wasn't my type. We both climbed the ladder in the loft with Randy holding the lantern. He had graduated just a year ago and in the iridescent lighting of the lantern, he was even better-looking. "Where are the kittens?" I asked, forgetting he wasn't my type.

He laughed as he probably thought, *The old kitten ploy. Gets them every time.* "Actually, there ain't any but until the power comes on or until your uncle gits back from visiting your auntie, we might as well take advantage of the sit-choo-ation."

He shut off the lantern, and I had my first kiss! The hay was a little damp but I let him lean me into a bale, and we kissed again and again. I knew enough to realize this must stop because it was bound to lead to trouble, but I couldn't resist those hot, blistering kisses.

Suddenly the stark darkness changed to brilliant light as

my uncle shined a huge flashlight on us. "So that's where you two are."

I said as casually as possible, "We were looking at kittens."

He chuckled, "Oh, so that's what you kids call it these days. I suggest you both get down. In case you haven't noticed, there's a major black-out due to a storm to the north when the sub-station got hit by lightning. That storm's headed our way and I need both of you to help me move the cows from the pasture to the barn."

I'll never forget where I was when the lights went out.

*lantern, iridescent, stark, damp, coincidence, broken, blistering, bound.

Toward the Light

Laura L. Hansen . *Poetry*

Through Every Broken Window

Through every broken window
leaves scurry like naughty mice,
rocks escape young boys' hands,
birds thrash their kamikaze feathers.

Below every broken window, glass
shards sparkle by daylight with
devilish gleam, threaten unprotected
feet, speak unspeakable dreams.

Beware the broken window, trust
shattering in an angry instant,
the falling tree wracked by wind
that brings the storm inside.

Through every broken window,
every broken promise, frost arrives
and chills the heart, beware the
hurling stone, the wedge of glass,

young boys—and fragile feathered
birds of love—will break your heart.

Dawn Loeffler . *Poetry*

Uncle Russel

I was walking through a market in Seattle, Washington
And there it was
So familiar
So delicious
Burnt chicory and sweet black cherry from his pipe
The instant feeling of family
Of rocking chairs
Sitting on his lap and laughter
Board games and passing food around the table in a circle
Tree houses and taxidermy ducks
Toy train tracks in a hidey-hole room tucked under the
        staircase
The way he could execute the cutting of a wooden rabbit
On the tabletop jigsaw without measuring
A long-eared, bushy-tailed souvenir of a childhood
So full of cousins
Enough for kickball, baseball, dodgeball
Acceptance by all ages
And there again, smell that?
Just a slight detection of dark cherry and chicory in the air
Uncle Russel all the way from Wisconsin to Washington
On the sea breeze
With a little smoke to cloud the frailty of memory

Georgia A. Greeley . *Poetry (Honorable Mention)*

1x0=0

Sitting alone at a table
in a restaurant

like the last beet
in a bowl

like the dog outside the door
wet, whimpering,

like the child not picked
for either team

like a young boy
forgotten by his mother

like a man
unable to touch another

like the match
too wet to light

like a single rock
on a beach, sinking in sand

Menu in hand, sealed in plastic,
a slickly worded list that offers

no sustenance.

Sue Bruns . *Poetry*

Torpor

Winter is the best time for love to die.

Alone on a winter's night, thermostat adjusted to
conserve, mind shut down,
body still, lost in a
shroud of bitter cold.
Suspended animation—
like birds in their mini-hibernation,
hypothermic sleep.

The heart does not stop but slows
to almost indiscernible beats.
Perched here with no thought
of hunger, no awareness
of cold or danger.

Winter nights are long.
Survival mode numbs
the senses, slows the pounding
heart. The mind goes
blank and forgets lost love.

Sheri Smith . *Creative Nonfiction*

Senior Citizen Grocery Store

I've slid into the seventh decade of my life and, as most people know, by the time we reach this age we are set in our ways and can be a bit cranky. Does "Get off my Lawn!" ring a bell? Since partying and raising kids is on the back burner, I have plenty of time to dream about what would make my life easier.

I would like a Senior Citizens Only Grocery Store. The main reason is for the safety of us Elders. No one under sixty-five years old is allowed for the following reasons. No teens racing carts down a crowded aisle or texting and running into the back of a fragile Achilles heel. No toddlers that we may mow over with our carts that are having the proverbial meltdown in the middle of an aisle. Our peripheral vision is not what it used to be.

Valet service would be a reality in my dream. Parking a block away from the main entrance has caused rapid heartbeats and pain in arthritic knees. If this is not feasible, I would like benches strewn around the parking lot, like confetti, as a resting spot for our weary bones.

Valet service should continue once we enter the store. I suggest supplying electric carts with a sidecar. The valets would be strapping young men and will be well-trained as to the location of all items in the store. Saving us precious time from roaming, backtracking, and confusion.

If valet service is not feasible, I then suggest changing the shelving. The lowest shelf should be two feet off the ground. Bending all the way to the current bottom shelf has induced a lower back spasm and a bout of dizziness upon returning upright. The upper shelves should be no higher than five feet. Seniors tilting their heads back and reaching upwards have been known to tip over. You might think this shelf arrangement may call for the grocery store to be twice the current size to accommodate the plethora of items currently stocked. I would glean out diapers, formula, bottles, rattles, nylons, sugary cereals, items that only come in huge quantities, multiple varieties of pop, and just five types of bread would make the store size manageable.

It would also help the store layout, and continue my dream, if products came in smaller sizes. Purchasing the smallest catsup which is only consumed on fries, tater tots, or added to an occasional sauce, has still gone way past the Best By date and has in fact solidified. Providing products in mini containers will save a ton of plastic waste each year, can be gripped by arthritic hands and will be consumed quicker. This will require a repurchase which will fuel the economy and the store's coffers as well as save the planet. I would also like to add a small area for those of us who use going to the grocery store as a social outing. A free doughnut and coffee bar would be most welcome. An area where we could meet new people, say hi to old friends, and consume a treat as a reward for getting this dreaded task completed.

Once at the checkout, a "Senior Discount" would be applied, as we are all on fixed incomes and food prices have gone insane. Side hustles to earn more cash only appeals to a small portion of us. Fifty-five years of working have left us content to sit home and read.

Lastly the valet would take me to my car, load the groceries, and wish me a pleasant day. As this whole scenario is an Elder's dream, if I give him a generous tip, I would also like him to drive me home, unpack the car, shelve the groceries, and make me a tasty meal.

I can dream, can't I?

James Walsh . *Creative Nonfiction*

Pickles vs. The World

Pickles shuffled into the meeting room, a walking glazed doughnut in Carhartt, crackling with each step. As was Ranger custom, real first names were dispensed with in favor of whatever nickname had overtaken it, so Pickles it was—not Jamie. The water main break, courtesy of Murphy's Law, had happened earlier that morning when temperatures had plummeted to minus twenty. In charge of water, sewer, street-sweeping, and practically anything else you can think of in small town Minnesota, Pickles had been first on the scene and gotten drenched in the process, rapidly turning into a human popsicle. Now he strode towards the table in the dimly lit Taconite city hall conference room, carrying with him a shroud of cold air like a passing phantom, arms slightly extended due to their icy bondage. His coverall coating was slowly undergoing a phase change from solid to liquid, like a real-time science experiment.

"How's everyone doing?" asked the man whose core temperature must have been hovering near the critical zone.

"Good, Pickles. How 'bout you?" I responded, eyeing his thawing carapace, arms slowly lowering to a neutral position.

"Oh, this here? Ah, just a water main break. Always happens on the coldest days, wouldn't cha know?" he said, shaking his head and grinning. Real doughnuts on the well-worn table were no challenge for his limited mobility, having devoured two before pleasantries had been completed. On the walls, sepia-toned photos from the turn of the century showed the town in its heyday, scions of its founding peering judgingly at the meeting participants.

The town was built on iron ore, and if there were any doubts about that the photographic evidence in the meeting room, the piles of rusty mine tailings surrounding the village, and even the town's name made it abundantly clear. Now, mines sat silent— any remnant equipment rusting like the tailings, main street businesses shuttered, the Spur station on the corner the only sign of commercial life.

"So, what's this meeting all about?" Pickles inquired, clearly trying to balance it mentally with other priorities.

As the joke goes, I was from the government, and here to help. "Well, it's about your water supply plan. Just gotta make sure everything's on track."

"Oh, right, forgot about that. Well, let's get on it."

We dug into the details, the regulatory requirements, the lofty goals for protecting their water supply over the next ten years.

"Ten years? Hell, by then we might all be taking dirt naps!" Pickles replied, sheepish grin spreading over his tired face. It was hard to argue against his logic.

"Ha, well, that may be so, but we're required to do it all the same," I replied, blending the duties of my job with an acknowledgment of his practical wisdom.

"How about we do what we can and then go from there?" Pickles offered—as reasonable a suggestion as one can imagine.

"Yes, I think that's what we're trying to arrive at with this document."

"Well, okay then," he said with a noble sincerity.

Flipping through the pages of the city's plan, I almost put myself to sleep and can only imagine what effect it was having on Pickles and others at the table. But they watched and listened with what seemed to be genuine, if not enthusiastic, interest. Moments later, as I reached my rousing conclusion, the conference room door burst open, the backhoe operator also covered in ice frantically searching the room.

"Hey, Pickles, we got a problem!" he bellowed, in what appeared to be a significant understatement.

"Guys, I gotta go. But lemme know what needs doing, and I'll get it done." With that, the meeting drew to an abrupt end and Pickles moved briskly away from the table. Door slamming behind him, he disappeared in a blanket of mist as his still-dripping coveralls met the blast of icy air.

Cindy Fox . *Poetry*

First Family Picture

Mother, eighteen years old, stylish in a curly bob wearing a button-down knee-length dark coat, tapered at the waist, Mary Jane heels strapped at the ankle, her left arm wrapped around Dad's waist. The other hand in her pocket.

Dad, twenty-seven years old, hair slicked back, in a white shirt and tie, dress pants and a leather jacket zipped half-way up, fitted snug at his Army-fit waist, his right arm draped around Mother's shoulder.

Hometown brick high school in the background.

Mother and Dad—they haven't met any of us yet.

Vicky A. King . *Poetry (Honorable Mention)*

Weightless

It's Fall.
The trees begin a slow strip-tease
relieving themselves of baggage.
Once fat with mid-life nonsense,
Esther's place did the same.
Its sides sucked in
like ancient cheeks.
The white clapboard thirsty for paint.
Her red maple hosting angry birds at
empty feeders.

As Esther's maple holds fast to
one last leaf,
in a mobile chair framed with chilled metal,
her body a weightless display,
her hair in need of a barrette,
her eyes vacant and cloudy.
Confined within barren walls,
her pleading spirit reaches for the heavens.

JJ Harrigan . *Creative Nonfiction*

Thanks for the Memory

By age twelve, Jack had lost his zest for hanging out with his grandparents. But the chance to tour the St. Paul fire station, where his uncle Tom served as a firefighter and paramedic, was too much to resist. So, on a Saturday morning in August, with an eager grin, Jack set out with my wife and me for the station. Just as we arrived, it looked as though our visit would be aborted. Horns blared, lights flashed, and sirens screamed as two fire trucks lumbered out of the garage. I pulled behind them, and Jack leaned forward. Watching his uncle fight a fire might fascinate him more than touring the station house. He clenched his jaw when we had to stop for red lights that the fire trucks plowed through. Far ahead of us, they turned onto side streets, and we lost them. My grandson's lips turned down in disappointment as we gave up the chase and returned to the firehouse to await their return.

When the firefighters got back, our son Tom toured us through the station. He pointed out the tower where long hoses hung to dry, the kitchen where one of the crewmen was preparing what looked to be an elaborate meal, and the exercise room where he let his nephew use the equipment. We went upstairs to see the fire pole poking through the floor. The pole was a magnet, and Jack's eyes shone as he reached for it. But Tom waved his finger. Only certified fire fighters were permitted to slide down the pole, and Jack would have to wait for another day. Then, to show him what he had to look forward to, Tom grinned and slid down the pole himself.

We trudged down the steps to the trucks in the garage. Tom put a helmet on Jack's head, draped a big, rubberized coat over his shoulders, and handed him an axe.

"This is heavy," said the twelve-year-old, struggling under the weight of the gear.

We climbed into the ambulance to see a bewildering array of paramedic equipment. Tom attached wire leads to Jack's chest and ran an EKG. A printer spit out a long tape showing a graph of his heart rhythms.

"Great readings." Tom smiled.

The captain invited us to ride in the fire truck. We piled in, and the truck pulled into the quiet East Side streets. The driver turned on the siren which made an ear-splitting screech inside the cab. Jack covered his ears, then laughed when a car in front of us pulled to the curb, thinking we were on a fire call.

The captain turned off the siren so we wouldn't annoy any more drivers, and we continued our short trip through the neighborhood. Tom put a plastic firefighter's hat on the boy's head and beamed with pride at his nephew as we left to go home.

Wearing the helmet, Jack marched up to his house and handed his mother the EKG printout.

"This was the best day of my life," he said.

Of course, you don't stay a wide-eyed twelve-year-old forever, and Jack is now in the Navy, training to work on the nuclear propulsion systems of aircraft carriers. His uncle, my son Tom, died shortly after our visit, entrapped in a wave of violence that swept the cities. The raw pain of that blow never disappears, but it helps to recall sweet moments of the past. And one of my fondest is that magical Saturday morning when son and grandson bonded at the firehouse.

Thanks, guys, for the memory.

Mary Kay Rummel . *Poetry*

Poet On a Blue Road

She moves her pen
instead of sleeping

Instead of throwing herself face-down
on a stone floor, vowing
to live with a god

She writes her visions before she forgets—

A single raindrop crowning
a tufted bronze foxtail

The cobalt road
nobody else has ever walked
or even dreamed of

Pagan odor of violets in church, clotted roots
just dug from earth

Her voice tender as a sinking moon,
one cloud
hypnotizing

So that we somehow *hear*
eternity in her words

Sharon Harris . *Poetry*

At Work

there are days when
life is just too cumbersome
when thoughts weigh me down
like massive stones
there are days when
truth lies hidden
when hope and lightness
are invisible

on those days
when I am careening
from one ponderous task
to another
I have no guidance
when the ones in control
all disagree

I need to find some place
out in the open air
where everything is clear
as a trout stream
cascading down a mountain
where burdens lift away
on vibrant wings
where the chores
are not so grievous

and my time is my own

Audrey Kletscher Helbling . *Creative Nonfiction*

Birthing Everett

Sometimes a mother just knows, feels an ache so deep in her bones that she can't sleep.

On January 16, 2025, I was that sleepless mother as my second-born daughter labored to deliver her son four hours away in a Madison, Wisconsin, hospital. Miranda was closing in on twenty-four hours of labor when I slipped beneath the covers. Sleep proved elusive as I tossed and turned.

An hour passed, then another and another, the digital numbers of the clock glowing red in my bedroom. I'd turned off my cellphone, instructed my son-in-law to call the landline in case of an emergency. Prophetic words.

I eventually fell into a fitful sleep, my troubling thoughts unable to completely shut off. It was as if my daughter was calling for me in her pain.

With the rising sun, I rose, switched on my smartphone. Wondering. Still worried. And then, just as my husband Randy was about to leave for work, the phone rang. A video call from our daughter. And there she was, holding her son. All ten pounds of him. A big boy birthed by a tiny-framed mama. Miranda looked exhausted, understandable after a long and difficult labor and delivery.

There were complications, Miranda and John shared. Bleeding and a need for three units of blood. "Don't worry, Mom, everything's okay now." I almost believed my daughter if not for her pale appearance and the sense that she was withholding information. Sometimes a mother just knows.

But in that moment, with darling Everett in her arms, I decided not to ask questions, to simply bask in the joy of a new grandson. Answers would come later. Each day we video-chatted. I couldn't get enough of the sweet baby boy I'd "seen" when accompanying Miranda to an ultrasound appointment months earlier. We laughed then about a single strand of spiking hair. But here he was, full head of black hair.

Eight days later, Randy and I were on the road to Madison. We'd waited until the new parents were home from the hospital, semi-settled and ready to have us. We packed the van with gifts, hand-me-down baby clothes, homemade frozen meals, suitcases and more. Upon arrival, I carried a load into the house, shed my coat, embraced my daughter, and asked to see my grandson.

In the upstairs nursery, we stood next to the crib, arms wrapped around one another, gazing down upon sleeping Everett. It's one of those moments I will forever cherish. Love times three.

Later, when we'd settled into the living room, Miranda and John shared details about Everett's birth, how his shoulder and head got stuck. How, after his birth, the fight was on to save Miranda. "We need to save her life!" the lead doctor shouted, instructing a room full of doctors and nurses to do everything they could to stop extensive postpartum hemorrhaging.

There was blood everywhere, John said. And my strong, strong daughter said she feared she would die.

The visual of that moment traumatized me in a way that only a mother can experience. That my daughter faced death in giving life proved almost too emotional to manage. Our hugs that day were fierce and long. Tears flowed. And I held my precious grandson Everett close, undeniably thankful his mother, my precious daughter, had lived to see him. To hold him, to love him, to tell me the story of how she nearly died on the morning he was born.

Cindy H. Kolling . *Poetry*

The winter wind howled

The day's light was done.
Gray skies spit flying pellets.
Hooded face shielded, the car left running,
he hurried, hunched over.
This would not take long.
Unseen, unheard, unnoticed, he hurried.
Through the alley, between the
dark garage and the little house.
He preferred to be less rushed.
He did not like to be pushed.
He'd rather do this differently.
Face to face was more his style,
but time urged him on.
The cold was setting in, the wind increasing.
He had it to do, and it would be done.
He reached the darkened step
at the back of the little house.
No one would see. No one would know.
He'd be done after this. Until the next time,
when he'd do it more properly.
He rang the doorbell.
She must have been waiting.
She may have been watching.
She probably was wondering.
She opened the door.
Wearing a robe, she stood in the wind.
In the bluster, he stood on the step.
He reached inside his long, heavy coat.
Without a word, he handed over the bag.
With a nod, he turned and disappeared into the dark.
White exhaust from his running car
mixed with the swirling snow.
Next time, he'd try to stay for coffee . . . but tonight,
just delivering the meals would have to do.

Kathleen J. Pettit . *Poetry*

Rerun

Fog like a lover's fingers caressed his hair
       as she lay next to him whose
       very breath powered her heartbeat.
Rivulets of sorrow lined her face,
       her silent scream a plea in the hollow of the night
       against the rising waters streaming toward his death.
She wills that each day left them
       be filled with the peace of acceptance.
But she knows what will happen next.
She has been here before.
Solace comes only from the sound of leaves
       brushing against each other as
       fingerlings of rain on windows
       slowly marked the minutes till dawn.

Roxanne Lien . *Creative Nonfiction (Honorable Mention)*

The Naughty Shoes

I eagerly awaited the arrival of my package after an online shopping spree. Nervously, I tore through the pink tissue paper. I held up one of the stilettos. The extravagant price and shoes made me feel a little naughty. The velvet suede was smooth and wickedly soft to the touch. I slipped the leopard print stilettos on each yearning foot and posed like Betty Grable in my full-length mirror. I stood in silence and found myself in a dream-like state; there were those long legs that men once admired, and once again, I was twenty-five and dancing across the floor of the Rainbow Room in NYC.

"God, you've still got it," I whispered, drinking in the glamour days of yesteryear.

In the other room, the phone rang, disrupting my peacock-preening. I answered it only to hear a nasal-voiced woman leaving a message from my doctor. *This is a reminder— your colonoscopy is scheduled for Friday afternoon.* Shit.

I turned back to the full-length mirror and confronted the reality of my seventy-three-year-old self. My fat, dimpled knees and varicose veins made the shoes look ridiculous, and my doctor told me I had lost two inches of my height, so the long, sexy legs were a thing of the past. My hands trembled as I replaced the expensive leopard stilettos in the box. "What was I thinking? I'm not wicked; I'm just delusional."

I'm embarrassed to report I now have two pairs of naughty shoes. My senior living facility was having its Christmas party; the silver glittery stilettos I had ordered arrived a week before. They're beautiful, and I proudly show them to the ladies at coffee one morning. They reminisce about their favorite pair of naughty shoes as their wrinkled fingers slide across the opulent silver stilettos. One friend said, "I could never stand up in those, let alone walk."

I explained, "I don't plan on wearing them. I've decided to

buy a pair of naughty shoes every year to have in my closet as a reminder of the young woman who once danced across the floor of the Rainbow Room."

Adrian S. Potter . *Poetry*

Dear Muse—

Trapped thoughts echo within my skull like a seashell with an ocean churning inside it. After you ditched me at the altar, I scoured the internet for your whereabouts. Questioned strangers until my tongue swelled with longing. Craved martinis and the salt from gin-drenched olives. O my thirst trap door. My corrupted metaphor. When you headed west wearing your highest heels, I searched in every karaoke bar from here to Vegas. Grumbled during the long drives between Podunk towns. Found you puking in an alley while confessing to petty crimes. On good days, you're the missing catalyst to my bootleg alchemy. On bad, a vixen with a box cutter at my neck. I put out a glass of chardonnay to tempt you. Leave behind trails of half-baked schemes and mistaken eureka moments. You hide my car keys and then threaten to riot. Flirt with the neighbor across the street, and toss my record collection in the trash out of spite. On good days, you coax me into lying on the floor while you chant *light as a feather, stiff as a board*. You help me levitate to new heights until I recognize your parlor trick for the con it is. So, you skip town, and in time, I track you down again. Our relationship remains tragically toxic. Symbiotic. Authentic.

Jeanne Everhart . *Poetry*

Ways of Looking at a Cat

Her spirit caressed the spirit
of one who thought
he despised cats; and won

Her Attabiah coat glistens
scrumptiously clean as
the kitten licks her mittens

I feel the soft song
the feline's silken body sings
vibrating and warm

The cat sits silent, with hooks
     set,
stealthily, like grey mist
the ungloved cat can steal
the voice of the blackbird

Her gemstone Pharaoh eyes
hold golden mysteries
in the daystar
and the hunter's moon

O Goddess Bastet of Egypt
you were, and are
elaborately pampered
in death and life

Who owns who—
do we exist
the cat for me
or me for the cat

Lorie Yourd . *Poetry*

A Yellow Bird

lies motionless on the deck. After a startling sound of impact at the window, I do not want to find this. Sometimes, birds are resilient after such accidents, and manage to recover—that hope is gone.

I must attend to it, but another bird is perched on the railing. The blue jay edges slowly toward the place where the goldfinch lies, peeping as it moves. Though my head knows these are not sounds of mourning, my heart recognizes empathy. The jay, still peeping, leaves the railing and alights next to the tiny body—a brief vigil, before it flies away.

The phone is ringing, and I let it go to the answering machine. I hear your voice inviting anyone calling to leave a message at the sound of the beep. "Here comes the beep," you say. This recording is one of few you left behind.

I carry the yellow bird to a place among trees, the air filled with avian calls. As I leave the thicket, I think of you, remembering the time I said you were a song in my soul.

"The talking stick is a Native American tradition used to facilitate an orderly discussion. The stick is made of wood, decorated with feathers or fur, beads or paint, or a combination of all. Usually speakers are arranged in a talking circle and the stick is passed from hand to hand as the discussion progresses. It encourages all to speak and allows each person to speak without interruption. The talking stick brings all natural elements together to guide and direct the talking circle." —Anne Dunn

This year, we received over 275 submissions from 119 writers. From these, the Editorial board selected 71 poems, 27 creative nonfiction stories, 12 fiction stories, and 18 creative twist entries for publication.

Please submit again!

www.thetalkingstick.com
www.jackpinewriters.com

Without the following contributors in 2024, this
Talking Stick would not have been possible.
Thank you to everyone!

Benefactors

Sue Bruns
Jeanne Cooney
Phyllis Emmel
Cindy Fox
Marlys Guimaraes
Marcus Kessler
Joni Norby
Niomi Rohn Phillips

Good Friends

Jeanne Everhart
Judith Feenstra
Meridel Kahl
James Robert Kane
Vicky A. King
Susan McMillan
Donna Uphus
Susan Niemela Vollmer

Special Friends

Sharon Chmielarz
Deborah Rasmussen
Cathy Wood

Friends

Nicole Borg
Joanne Cress
Victoria Smith

Anthony Anselmo
MBL Birch
Janice Larson Braun
Sue Bruns
Sharon Chmielarz
Jan Chronister
Amelia Colwell
Dan Crouser
Judy Daniel
Norita Dittberner-Jax
Charmaine Pappas Donovan
Sandra Hughes Eberhart
Joanne Esser
Jeanne Everhart
Cindy Fox
Shelley Getten
Georgia A. Greeley
Marlys Guimaraes
Tara Flaherty Guy
Laura L. Hansen
JJ Harrigan
Sharon Harris
Margaret Hasse
Audrey Kletscher Helbling
Jennifer Hernandez
Donna Isaac
Carolyn Jacobs
Meridel Kahl
James Robert Kane
Charles Kausalik-Boe
Vicky A. King
Cordelia Kochmann
Cindy H. Kolling
Laura Krueger-Kochmann
Janet Kurtz
Kristin Laurel
Mike Lein
Roxanne Lien

Steve Linstrom
Gail Lipe
Jayna Locke
Dawn Loeffler
Linda Maki
Chris Marcotte
Alice Springer Marks
Erin Lynn Marsh
Susan McMillan
Ryan M. Neely
Constance Neumiller
Ann Marie Newman
Joni Norby
Yvonne Pearson
Kathleen J. Pettit
Niomi Rohn Phillips
Adrian S. Potter
Rebecca Rae
Deborah Rasmussen
Kit Rohrbach
Mary Kay Rummel
Dorothy Schlesselman
Jodi Schwen
Richard Fenton Sederstrom
Sheri Smith
Laura Syrdal
Dawn Tanner
Bernadette Hondl Thomasy
Tammy Tisdell
Kara Tollerud
Peggy Trojan
Steven R. Vogel
Susan Niemela Vollmer
James Walsh
Elizabeth Weir
Pamela Wolters
Cathy Wood
Lorie Yourd